THE FOURTH
PRINCESS

THE FOURTH PRINCESS

Eileen L. Maschger

ReadersMagnet, LLC

The Fourth Princess
Copyright © 2022 by Eileen L. Maschger

Published in the United States of America
ISBN Paperback: 978-1-956780-94-9
ISBN eBook: 978-1-956780-93-2

All rights reserved. No part of this publication may be reproduced, stored in a retrieval system or transmitted in any way by any means, electronic, mechanical, photocopy, recording or otherwise without the prior permission of the author except as provided by USA copyright law.

The opinions expressed by the author are not necessarily those of ReadersMagnet, LLC.

ReadersMagnet, LLC
10620 Treena Street, Suite 230 | San Diego, California, 92131 USA
1.619. 354. 2643 | www.readersmagnet.com

Book design copyright © 2022 by ReadersMagnet, LLC. All rights reserved.
Cover design by Kent Gabutin
Interior design by Renalie Malinao

For my family and friends who empower me, my children who enliven me, and my husband who encourages me.

Chapter

Once upon a time there was a beautiful kingdom. It was ruled by a king who was extremely wise, and worked hard to serve all who dwelled there. His constant vigilance toward his kingdom ensured its strong prosperity. No kingdom is perfect. Even if one was, there is bound to be a constant supply of greedy neighboring kingdoms. There are also residents who try to reach out their slippery hands to take away all the king has worked hard to establish. Keeping this kingdom as strong and great as it was, was no small task. Its magnificence endured through the wisdom and determination of its mighty king. Every villainous plot conceived was quickly thwarted by the king. To those who have never met the king, he was believed to be blessed with the ability to foresee the future. However, those who knew him better attributed this prosperity to his superb application of logic before making any rash decisions.

The queen was lovely. You would not notice her beauty at first. In fact, were it not for her royal attire, she could easily be dismissed as any other mature woman her age. The queen had a beauty that emanated from her heart, which excused any physical flaw some would pick out. She was a shining example of love, comfort and understanding. It also wouldn't take long for you to realize she was every bit as clever as her husband. Unlike the king, her strength was not in facts, but in creativity. She smiled more, sang more and was the perfect balance for the king and kingdom. Together they were a strong force to be reckoned with; and as one, kept their kingdom safe.

The royal family had four beautiful princesses. Each had grown up with an extensive staff of extraordinary tutors that taught a wide range of subjects. The eldest, Princess Lydia, studied hard and became the smartest of all the princesses. At times her thoughts even rivaled the king's. This pleased the king and queen. As the heir to their kingdom they were happy she was wise and began to include her in discussions of kingdom affairs. She sat in on various matters of business and was molded into a formidable leader for the kingdom. The extra attention pleased the princess, and she was delighted her parents were proud of her as their daughter.

The second princess, Princess Dianna, was nothing like the eldest. She hated studying. Oh, she knew how to read and understood what she was being taught. She simply was bored by it. Each day, she would count down every passing moment in the library until it was time for her lessons on combat training. She enjoyed the movement of the sword in her hand, the bow drawn tight, and the slide of her feet as she deflected each attack. Through the years she became stronger and quicker with each weapon. Accuracy was never a question. She always knew exactly when and where to strike. Dianna never missed. Yet, with all her disdain, she still remained faithful to her other studies. She realized the knowledge gleaned would only help her become a better leader for her troops as well as her kingdom. This pleased the king and queen. They knew she would make an excellent queen who would protect her kingdom with all her heart. The princess couldn't be happier; she knew her parents were proud of her talent and hard work.

The third princess, Princess Melissa, endured her studies just like her sisters. What was special about Melissa was her miraculous beauty. Even as a baby, friends, family, diplomats, even servants would comment on her radiance. The older she grew the more dazzling she became. When she spoke everyone would listen, hanging on her every word. Her parents and tutors still encouraged her to keep learning, and she quickly realized there was no point in having everyone listen to her if she had nothing good to say. This pleased the king and queen. They knew she would never want for suitors, and she would be smart enough to choose a good Prince to rule alongside. The princess was also happy because she knew her parents were proud of her as their daughter.

The fourth princess, well, let's just say she had no obvious skill. Being the youngest she wanted to work hard to keep up with her amazing sisters. She studied her lessons vigorously, but always came up short compared to Lydia's intellect. She practiced the sword and many other battle skills; again, never as good as Dianna. She tried to take great care of her appearance, and practiced all the rules of etiquette a princesses should know. However, she could never match the grace and splendor of dear Melissa. She eventually became versed in many subjects, trying to find out her unmistakable talent. She wanted so desperately to please her parents the same way her sisters had. But, in every way, she was merely "sufficient" in her work; not gifted. The king and queen were confused by their daughter's results. They presumed she may not be trying hard enough in her studies, and encouraged her to remain diligent. Her sisters tried to cheer her up with games and treats that were always accompanied by words of advice.

"They are simply worried about your future. Don't you want to be in a good kingdom that you can rule with confidence and wisdom like them?" Princess Lydia would always say.

"They are just worried you will be outwitted in battle. A random assassin could easily catch you unaware, and the next thing you know you're dead after choking on your own blood." Princess Dianna would remind her.

"They worry no one will want to marry you because you don't exercise the proper amount of charm that every princess needs to attract a prince." Princess Melissa would prod.

Her family believed the way to "sugar coat" brutal advice was to actually give you a sugary treat before they spoke harsh truths that you needed to face. The little princess did not shy from those truths and continued to work exceptionally harder in her studies. But, she knew it was all in vain when her parents started using phrases around her like:

"Too young."

"Time to grow up."

"You will get it eventually."

Their remarks brought her down lower and lower until she found it hard to smile at anything. She felt like she was a disappointment to her entire family regardless of her best efforts. With all her hard work, nothing she did was good enough.

As you may have guessed, years of comments like these will take its toll on any person, especially a little princess. As time went by she found herself spending less time with her sisters and more time stuck in a stuffy library with piles of books she was expected to study. With every passing day her tutors became more upset with her obvious failure, and their haughty attitudes reflected it. Instead of encouraging understanding and passion from the little princess. They jumped from subject to subject in the hopes that, "Today would be the day the Princess reveals her true gift." The older she grew the more she would hide to avoid each dreary lesson. First she would hide in her rooms. When she was found there, she moved on to the kitchens. The princess was pretty good at hiding in the vast castle gardens, but eventually she would be found and escorted to the library. When there was nowhere else to hide she ventured out of the castle entirely. She was nervous at first, but the nearby city proved to be filled with all the delights and excitement that her family's castle lacked. The princess leapt at any opportunity to become involved in a project. Harvesting, building, sewing, cleaning, cooking; if someone needed help, she would race toward the opportunity. Anything to get her out of her lessons for a little longer. She learned the perfect place to hide was in a crowd, and what was more crowded that the nearby village? In the crowd she felt safe, she knew even if her tutors knew where she was they would never venture in after her. In the crowd she was… free.

 The princess grew to love the people in her kingdom. She laughed with them, cried with them, celebrated and mourned with them. She became known as the "People's Princess", though no one uttered the phrase too loudly. One unguarded comment to the wrong person and as quick as a flash palace guards would appear to retrieve the princess, then drag her back to those dusty books. Those were the days they would punish her with extra work with an unbiased eye on her.

 Years flew by and the four little princesses were not so little anymore. The lovely Princess Melissa was married to a fair prince, equal in beauty and mind. The king permitted the princess to choose her own husband. Every prince who sought her hand in marriage was considered to be a good match in the king's mind, so her final decision did not concern him at all. She was happy with her decision. And so, Melissa's "happily ever after" started as she accompanied her prince to his palace in a faraway kingdom.

Not long after that blessed event, Princess Dianna, strong and independent, was married to a young king. Many thought she would marry a man just as versed with battle schemes as she. Although the king was a powerful man, he was tender and romantic toward Dianna in every way. He was a perfect figure of restraint and tact, and together, they were unwavering force. Dianna's "happily ever after" began as she left the palace to her new life, with her new king.

The eldest, Princess Lydia, swore she would never marry until she was sought out by a worthy companion of her dreams, who was equal to her in every way. Many suitors tried to win her heart, but none were her equal in logic and wisdom. She continued to assist in affairs of the kingdom until her parents conceded she was a powerful ruler – with or without a husband. And so, the kingdom was formally passed on to her. Her "happily ever after" began when her mother's crown adorned her head.

Chapter

Watching her sisters move on to happier and better lives filled the youngest princess with joy. Unfortunately, her happiness for her sisters melted away swiftly as she began to wonder when her own life would change for the better. After days and days of studying and waiting, she grew tired of sitting around and resolved to do something about it herself. And then, a thought came to her as clear as a morning sunrise in spring.

"Maybe," she thought, "my destiny is not to lead, but to assist those who do? I'm not an expert at anything, but I do know a little about almost everything. I'm sure I could be fairly helpful."

She straightway went to her older sister to offer her services. Queen Lydia was delighted to have her around. She was happy her little sister had finally decided to show some initiative with her studies, and she was put to work right away. Initially, it was a great day. The little princess was happy to fetch her sister things, be ready with particular documents, as well as recording summaries of each audience seen by the queen. Eventually the little princess felt comfortable enough to make her own changes regarding her sister's work. Protocol and order were thrown out the window as the youngest princess would rush to get the work done. She missed the old times when she and her sister could enjoy good fun together. The Princess wanted to finish the work, so they could enjoy some time together again. When the queen found out, she was virulent with rage. She liked everything in its place and accounted for, not rushed and messy. The little sister grew more and more "in the way" as Lydia worked, and they both decided her services were no longer needed.

The youngest retreated to the garden heartbroken and embarrassed. She tried to find some peace as she soaked up the last little bits of sunlight from the day. But, her sister had found her, and the princess immediately braced for a terrible scolding. Instead the queen had sat down next to her, and patted her sister's shoulder lovingly.

"Thank you." She spoke softly to her little sister. The little one was surprised, but still skeptical of what would come next. "Because of your... mess, we found an old set of plans that was sent to the palace years ago. It happened to be the solution to one of our major problems we have been unable to resolve lately. It wasn't a problem when we initially received the plans, so it was discarded in a room filled with other unused ideas. We may never have found it, if not for you." The youngest felt a little bit of pride that she had helped, even if it was accidentally. She allowed herself a small smile for her small accomplishment. The Queen continued, "I would like to offer you a position to serve as my royal scroll keeper. You would be in charge of organizing all discarded plans so, in the future, it will be easier to find possible solutions to pressing matters."

Her little sister bowed her head, honored by the offer. "That is a brilliant idea sister, but I fear there are more people qualified for this position than I. Besides, I can practically guarantee there will be more unwelcome accidents if we continue to work together."

Lydia smiled, "You make an excellent point, dear sister, but what will you do now?"

"Well, since I was able to help you, I think I will visit our sisters in their kingdoms. Perhaps I can help them as well."

"Just try not to make a mess of their work too." The queen said with a smile. "I will have a carriage ready for you in the morning."

For the first time in a while, the littlest princess went to bed happy that night.

*****

The trip to Princess Dianna's palace went faster than anticipated. The littlest princess' mind was a blaze of thoughts concerning how to help her sister. Before she had left her parent's castle, the king and queen had wished her luck and reminded her not to be disappointed if she wasn't much help in the end. They also reminded her there was no shame in returning home where she could be taken care of. The little princess could not shake this thought. Indeed, there will be plenty of shame in returning home without doing something extraordinary. The little princess wanted her parents to stop looking at her with worry and concerns. She wanted to be seen as someone just as special as any of her sisters. Everyone in her family had one special trait that they excelled at; she just had no idea what her special trait was… yet.

Queen Dianna met her at the front gate with a tight embrace. They were so happy to see each other as it had been quite a while since Dianna left to start her new life with her husband. Together again, the two sisters wasted no time to catch up on recent events over large amounts of cookies and tea.

"Oh, how I wish I had seen her face when you made a mess out of all her rules and procedures!" Dianna laughed loudly when her younger sister tried to duplicate Lydia's face; beet red, veins bulging, lips disappearing. Even she couldn't do it without laughing.

"So, I decided to come here to see if I could help you out with anything."

Dianna choked a little on her tea. "Oh, well, we seem to be doing fairly well right now. I'm not sure how much help you will be. But I have missed sparring with you. Come, let's see what you have learned since I've been gone."

The sparring match was terribly one sided. The youngest was no match for the older, more disciplined sister. Clearly the queen was enjoying herself, as she had started to taunt and tease the little princess. She kept telling her sister to be more aggressive in her attacks, but when the words "prove yourself" touched her lips the little princess saw red. Years of built up anger was suddenly released in an explosive burst of energy. She lashed out at Dianna in a moment of pure, absolute rage. The queen was knocked to the floor and her sword had been broken in two. When the youngest sister realized what just happened, she dropped her sword in surprise. On the floor were scarlet drops of blood that had oozed from a shallow cut on her older sister's arm.

"Are you crazy?" shouted the queen, angry and confused. "Look what you have done to my sword!"

"I'm so sorry!" The little princess repeated over and over as she backed up closer to the exit. When she found an opportunity, she dashed from the room in complete embarrassment.

All day the little princess hid in the garden, not knowing where else to go. What had happened in there? She was not a better fighter than her sister. Not by a long shot. But, for the first time she actually defeated her. The small amount of pride that swelled in her chest quickly deflated when she remembered she had also broken her sister's sword. If there's one thing she knew, warriors and their weapons are one and the same. She could have cut off her sister's arm and gotten the same reaction from her. Now, she was scared. Scared of her sister, of what she would say, and most importantly scared of what she would do. Even worse, she was scared of the dreaded scolding her parents would give her once they found out what happened.

"There you are!" The queen strolled over and settled down nicely next to her sister. "You gave me quite a scare. I have never seen that much power from you, or should I say anger?"

All the princess could do was shake her head back and forth whispering "I'm sorry, I'm sorry..." over and over again. She didn't want to hear it. She didn't want to be yelled at. She couldn't bear to hear another lecture about how she had made the wrong decision, and should take better care of her actions. But, those weren't the words she heard.

The younger princess shook her head confused, "What did you say?"

"Pay attention, I don't say 'thank you' often." Snorted the queen.

"For what? I broke your sword. I cut your arm!"

"This? Oh, it won't even leave a scar. Not to worry, I have many brilliant healers close by to take care of scratches like these. Focus now. I'm thanking you for finding the weakness in my weapon. I showed it to my husband who took it to our blacksmith. Apparently he has an apprentice who has been working with different types of metals and the heating process in his spare time. They believe to have found a better steel for our armies. As we speak they are making me a new sword in this fashion.

"You would have met with this apprentice eventually, without my help."

"Perhaps, but you certainly sped things along, didn't you?" She scooted a little closer to her sister and whispered so only they could hear. "You may have saved my life. You taught me a lesson no instructor or trainee has ever come close to."

"What's that?"

"Random craziness." She said with a smile.

"Pardon me?"

"Random craziness. Everyone who has taught me has shown me forms, strategies, and made sure I took calculated risks. They taught me this way because that's how they think." The queen focused intently on her younger sister. The little princess blinked back at her, silently waiting for something to make sense.

The Queen continued, "You, however, stopped thinking for a moment. You weren't thinking about maneuvers, or risk, or what I would do. You simply attacked; no rhyme or reason to it. I was surprised and caught off guard. I learned to never underestimate my opponent. All the calculations in the world are no match for blind chaos."

"Thanks, I think." The little sister said with a smile.

"Stay with us here. I could use you to help train my troops. You're still much better at this than most of them."

"No. Like you said, you are doing well here and I fear I would only get in the way. Besides, I'm terrified every time you spar with me."

The queen laughed warmly at her sister, "As it should be!"

The princess told of her desire to visit Queen Melissa to see if she could be of some use there. A fresh carriage was summoned the next day and she was off on another journey.

*****

Before meeting with her sister, Melissa, the princess was escorted to a room where she was washed, perfumed, oiled and given a brand new dress to wear. A much more flattering and much more constricting dress. A servant led her to the throne room where Queen Melissa sat waiting for her entrance. A smile spread across the queen's lips as she descended her throne. The princess stared in wonder at how her sister managed to look like she was floating down the steps on a cloud of petticoats. The thought was dismissed as they embraced in a tender, yet delicate fashion. The youngest suspected the overly constricting dresses might have something to do with that. The Queen broke the silence first.

"I am so happy you finally decided to come see me!"

The little princess blushed "I'm sorry. Your kingdom was furthest away, so I thought I would visit Dianna first…"

"I had always hoped," Queen Melissa interrupted, "you would come to me one day. To finally forgo all those tutors and choose to learn from me directly about beauty and grace. I can show you so many skills that will help breathe new life into your rather ordinary canvas."

"Canvas?" They strolled down a palace corridor, passing many doors along the way. Exactly what was behind each door, the little princess could not imagine. She was too busy trying to understand what her sister wanted from her.

"You, of course! That is why you are here, for me to make you into the best YOU ever?"

"Well…"

"Of course you are. I will teach you myself what those finishing ladies whish they knew. When I am done with you, you will not even recognize yourself. What do you think?"

"Where do we start?" She wasn't sure why she spoke those words. Agreeing to more lessons of health and grooming was like sentencing the princess to the dungeons, infested with rats. She couldn't imagine how the nibbling and pawing of rats would feel much different than the poking and prodding of her sister's beauticians.

The older sister chuckled when she clapped her hands. A procession of servants armed with combs, brushes, salves, oils, scrubbers and many things the princess couldn't imagine why they would need, corralled her into a chair where they began their work.

"Here come the rats." Thought the poor princess.

When the pawing was over the little princess' skin was tingling in every possible crevice. Her sister said she was glowing, but that could be the brilliant red hue from her young skin now exposed from masterful scrubbings.

"Tomorrow, after your skin has rested, we will continue with the transformation."

After a long ride to the palace and a long day with her sister, the princess was ready for a nice long rest. Unfortunately, the meaning of the word tomorrow for her sister was: long before the sun hit the horizon. It was still dark in the little princess's room when Queen Melissa entered in all her beautiful perfection; ready to continue the work on her sister. The younger sister rubbed the sleep from her eyes baffled by the image of perfection looming next to her.

"What time did you need to get up, so you could look this perfect before sun rise?" She croaked at the queen a little too harshly.

"Beauty knows no time, dear sister." The queen answered as a bucket of water was poured over her little sister's head.

The morning was spent with several ladies pulling and rolling her dark brown hair into several different styles. After a few hours, Melissa stated the princess's hair flattered her most when it was off the shoulders. After that, the remaining time was spent pinning, clipping, folding and who knows what else to the little princess' hair. She couldn't recall exactly what they had done. What she did know, was all this hard work was giving her a terrible headache. For a brief moment she wondered if her sister was slowly poising her to death with lethal hairpins, but that was plain nonsense... wasn't it?

Next came an extremely small lunch, consisting of fruits and nuts. While still starving, the little princess was dragged into another room filled with an army of seamstresses to muse about what her new wardrobe should look like. She was dizzy with color swatches, measurements, tucks, and even more pins. Every other minute the princess was told to stand up straight by the seamstresses who tried not to be bothered by her casual stance.

The next day had been planned to coincide with an important meeting in which the queen would be showing off her lovely little sister. It all started early again with another washing, followed by an elaborate dress and hairstyling. When she was finished, the princess was shown to Queen Melissa's personal dressing room. She sat in front a large mirror hanging on a wall and a small table that held a rainbow of paints and powders. Her sister patted an empty chair next to her, inviting her to sit.

"This is my favorite part." She said while facing her own refection. "This is when we take the blank canvas and paint whatever we want on it. All your flaws, gone with a flick of a brush. Now, pay attention to what I do."

It had just occurred to the princess that this was the first time, since they were little girls, that she had not seen her sister all painted up. She didn't know how to react. Her sister wasn't ugly at all, but she did seem off in some way. The same way her mother looked before her first morning cup of chocolate. She watched intently, barely hearing what her sister was saying. The princess was so eager to try each stroke she decided to follow along instead of waiting. She picked up a brush.

The rest of the lesson was a blur of her sister correcting her, colors spilling, brushes snapping and teeth grinding in rage. Through it all, the little princess thought she looked pretty good.

The queen, on the other hand, had not planned on the lesson being so strenuous. Her colored powders were not applied in its usual perfection. In fact, the queen's face was a mess. Her hair was falling out of its style in pieces, and her dress was smeared with color from top to bottom.

"Look at me!" The queen was purple with rage as she directed her anger toward her little sister. "I can't convince the kingdom nearby their trade demands are absurd while looking like this!" The princess swallowed hard as Melissa grabbed a brush, turning to face the mirror. "Maybe I can quickly…"

"My queen," the king called as he entered the room. "It is time to entertain our guests."

"I cannot, my dear! They must wait! I'm not ready at all."

"Come now, matters such as these do not wait." The king held out his arm to his queen.

Melissa scowled at her sister as if to burrow into her mind the severity of her, actions. Reluctantly, she rose with all the grace she could muster, and joined her husband.

Once again the princess ran to hide, and once again she found the gardens. She climbed up one of the tallest trees and began devouring the lemons it bore on a nearby branch. The princess was just about to drift asleep when she heard her sister below.

"Lemons are terrible for your teeth!"

"So what? They are delicious! They are meant to be eaten, not squeezed over your hair to lighten it!"

"Come down from there."

"No, I'll only mess something else up."

"As you wish. I thought you should know, the agreement went better than anticipated."

"Congratulations," the princess mumbled. Her tone was flat and unimpressed.

"Because of you."

THE FOURTH PRINCESS

The little princess jumped down from the tree. She wasn't at all bothered by the stains on her brand new dress. Her sister; however, struggled to ignore each one.

"Our trade supplier saw me in a state I don't think he will ever want to see me in again. He must have thought I was disheveled and furious concerning his demands. He caved in like an underdone cake, and even offered extra in our next shipment for the grievances he had put us through."

"Really?" The princess was doubtful of the story. Three accidents resulting in three major triumphs. The odds were not there.

"I believe his exact words were, 'I never knew our agreement meant so much to you personally. Please, forgive me.' Grovel, grovel, beg, beg, beg… you get the idea."

"Wow," was all the youngest could manage to say. She was still stunned by her good fortune.

"You must stay and teach me all these different 'faces' to portray. Beauty will not last forever."

"I know there are many in your kingdom that can help you better than I can. I cannot stay. I understand now I need to live my own life."

"And what kind of life would that be?"

"Well, I enjoy helping, but I don't enjoy the critique that comes along with it as a princess."

The queen blushed, "Then, you must go into the world disguised. That way, you will never be judged as a proper princess would, and you aren't obligated to meet any more kings or queens. Unless you want to, of course."

The Fourth Princess smiled brightly. "I think it's time for a different kind of makeover, sister."

Chapter

M any years later. Far, far away where the weather is warmer and the water much more salty, existed another kingdom. A grand castle was nestled on the edge of a cliff which oversaw the tide coming in and out. It was a beautiful kingdom to live in, assuming the heat didn't bother you too much. Everyone who lived there believed their king to be strong and understanding. Whenever there was a problem, it was fixed; grievances were quickly resolved, and always in the king's name. They believed him to be a great man, but the real story inside the castle was another matter.

The king, was a great man; when he was younger. Unfortunately, age had not been kind to him. His brain didn't function as well as it used to. To put it bluntly, he was mad. Harmless for sure, but mad just the same.

THE FOURTH PRINCESS

The queen, was not much better. Unlike her husband, she was completely sane. However, she hated managing the affairs of her kingdom. "Mind-numbing nonsense!" she would often say when bothered with the latest news. She was much more concerned with tending her garden, eating rare delicacies and being entertained by performers of all kinds.

The prince, was the brains of the castle. He would lounge on the steps that led up to the king and queen's thrones casually listening to every report. He would make suggestions to his mother. Sometimes she repeated his idea to the messenger, but mostly would simply wave her had dismissing the "nonsense" without a word. This usually resulted in the messenger glancing at the prince who would give a small nod meaning, "Please try what I said." In this fashion, he ran the kingdom very well, but he always worked under the name of the king. Often, he would petition his mother to officially pass the crown onto him. However, it is hard to reason with anyone who does not want to listen. His petitions would always be ignored while his mother occupied herself with small matters, such as her garden.

So, if the prince was really the one running the kingdom, why didn't the people know about it by now? Surely there would be rumors, stories from the servants that would leak out of the castle and into the villages. Not in this kingdom. If there is one thing the queen despised, it was gossip. Royal gossip was the worst. All it took was one whisper, one word she did not approve of and it was immediately stamped out. The way this was done was thanks to a clever contraption one of the royal chefs had crafted to mash his ingredients in a much faster, more efficient pace. It was brilliant for fruit, nuts, potatoes, and tongues… yes, tongues. One day the queen heard a servant saying unspeakable things about the king. She was so angry, she snatched the man by his tongue and dragged him down to the kitchens. His tongue was inserted into the contraption and that was the end of that. The tongue is an amazing muscle in the human body. It is quite strong and resilient. When the mashing was over the poor servant still had his tongue, but it was bruised badly enough that it was hard to speak. Eventually it healed, and he was back to normal. But, after his ordeal; he never gossiped again. Thus the secret endured and the king's reputation stayed sound.

It was hard to live among such people. The prince usually was lonely and wanted to talk to someone about the happenings of the day. So, he spent most of his spare time with the fool who entertained the castle. He wasn't really a fool; he was a doctor. In fact, he was one of the best doctors money could find. He was brought in years ago when the king started to turn for the worse. Through the many treatments, the king slowly decided everything the doctor said was hilarious. When no further treatments worked, the doctor was asked to continue working at the castle; only now he was the fool.

Fool aside, the prince found his life to be rather dull and monotonous. Each day seemed to muddle into the net one. Even the rain brought no change for the prince's mood. The castle was dreary enough; why would the rain make any difference? But, on this particular night, the rain brought something that would shake up his life forever.

Chapter

The prince was lounging on his throne strumming his guitar to the melody of a slow waltz. He wasn't paying attention the music, however. His mind was adrift, dreaming away to pass the time. His parents had already retired for the evening; while most of the servants had long since finished their work and retreated to their rooms. It was late, but the prince hated to sleep. Sleep only made tomorrow come too fast for him. The last thing he wanted was to enable his dreary life to slip away more rapidly with his eyes shut. His solution was to avoid the sunrise as long as he could. Any given evening he could be found reading, exercising, and even writing. Today he was strumming to the rhythm of the rain.

KNOCK, KNOCK, KNOCK! The sound was so loud and sudden it shook the prince out of his seat! He looked around for a servant to appear, but he found none. They were all tucked away in their rooms. Honestly, who knocks at the front door of a castle anyway? KNOCK, KNOCK, KNOCK! The prince still could not believe what he was hearing. The hour was so late the poor prince wasn't sure what he should do. He continued to stare, motionless, at the door. It was the faint voice of a woman half drowned out by the rain that snapped him back to reality.

"Hello? Hello? Is anybody there?"

The prince scooted his way to the door. "Um, yes, I'm coming." He answered back, still uncertain.

The prince opened the door just a crack to find a woman with large brown eyes and dark hair. She was soaked and shivering from the cold, wet night; but on her face was still a dazzling smile as if she were the one receiving him.

"Hello! I'm so glad you answered. I was afraid everyone had gone to bed already. I am in terrible need of your help."

Still standing at the door, the prince managed a hesitant, "Um, yes, well, there are many homes in the village nearby that may be willing to help."

The woman blinked as she regarded him, then continued with her story. "I got lost in the rain and my horse was spooked by something, throwing me from his saddle. I started walking to find somewhere dry… are you going to invite me in?"

Still at a loss the Prince muttered, "I'm not sure I can… the… um…"

"You do live here, do you not?"

"Of course I do!"

"And you do know it's terribly rude to leave a visitor standing outside your door in the pouring rain, yes?"

That comment shook the prince back to normal. He blushed knowing full well he was being extremely rude, regardless who was at his door.

"Yes, of course. Please come in." She entered the dry, warm receiving room. But seeing her in a better light only confused the prince more.

She looked like any other lovely woman, except her hair was cut short, falling in layers around her face. It was one of the oddest things the prince had ever seen. Then he saw her clothes. Several types of leather were sewn together into a short jacket with a broad hood. As she unbuttoned it, he could see several pockets hidden among the outer seems and lining the inside as well. He recognized the shirt as a simple tunic and was happy to see traditional, feminine lace spilling around her loose, untied collar and wrists. That seemed normal to him except for a sturdy chain that hung around her neck. Again, not entirely unusual, but laced on the chain was a man's bulky ring that peeked out from behind the collar of her shirt. Her pants, yes pants, were sturdy and littered with buttons, hooks, and clasps of all sizes. He guessed each clamp was another pocket to hide things away in. On her feet were sturdy military boots laced up to her knees. He also saw a hint of a knife hiding in the side of one boot. This only make him wonder what else she may be hiding on her, and where?

"Thank you so much kind sir, are you aware how thick the mud is out ther? Well, I was walking and my leg got sucked into a mud hole, and I twisted my ankle trying to get it out. I wasn't sure what to do, until I saw your door! I knew if I made it here I would be alright."

"My dear… woman," he wasn't quite sure what to call her. "Do you know where you are?" His tone was arrogant and a bit insulted.

"Like I said, I'm lost. I have no idea where I am. Please, can you help me?"

"You are at the royal palace in the Kingdom of Tridith, home of King Theodore!" The prince tried not to be bothered, but it was very late and his patience was wearing thin.

She looked around the room, taking in the entire atmosphere. "No kidding! I must say I am quite impressed. This is one of the grander receiving rooms I've been in. Now, will you please help me with my ankle?"

The prince scoffed at her, "You are asking me, the prince, to help you with your ankle?" He couldn't believe the lack of respect she had towards him. He has never been treated this way in his life!

"Oh my goodness, the prince! I am honored to meet you." She curtsied, but it looked rather strange. Not strange because of her hurt ankle, strange because he was used to seeing this done with long flowing skirts. She held out her hand to him. "I am, The Fourth Princess. Thank you for receiving me."

"Princess?" he spat out as he started to chuckle. She simply looked back at him with a flat, practiced smile.

"It seems compassion is lacking in this kingdom. My father would have paddled me until I was red for laughing at a poor, injured traveler."

The prince tried to compose himself while wiping tears from his eyes. "I'm sorry. It's just… I mean, you don't really expect me to…" She stared at him with a stone look. The small, practiced smile still remained, but her eyes shot ice that dared him to finish his sentence. The prince swallowed hard and shifted his feet. "…expect me to make you wait much longer to have your ankle looked at."

Her smile became genuine again. "Thank you so much. I knew you would help me. I apologize for my appearance. It's hard to look glamourous every hour of every day, especially after being caught in the rain."

He held out his arm to escort her to a room she would be comfortable in. More specifically, he was escorting her to a room his mother would never find her in. He wasn't sure why he suddenly felt the need to treat her as an equal. It just seemed wrong not to do so. He tried to find something he could say without sounding like an idiot.

"So, interesting attire you're wearing. Were they made for traveling?"

"Yes and no. My sister mentioned I needed to appear more aggressive, so people wouldn't underestimate me. So, I fashioned an outfit based on the under armor a soldier would wear."

The Prince knew a good soldier had many layers of padding that was worn under the metal armor. Now that she said something, he could see the similarities. Close to the body, but free moving. There were patches that reinforced the forearms and soft spots on the chest and back. She was one suit of armor short from being ready for a war.

"Well, it definitely catches one off guard. But, why so many pockets?"

"My sister taught me to always have my things organized and within close reach. I am constantly on the move so I travel light. Everything I really need is on me in some way. Cuts back on extra weight and keeps my mind focused on more important things."

The prince couldn't help but nod in understanding. Everything she said made sense even though he was still shocked by her appearance. The more she spoke, the more questions he had for her. Another feeling in the back of his head encouraged him to not pry too deep, too fast. "Would it be out of line if I asked what happened to your hair?"

"Do you like it? It's a bit extreme, but my sister mentioned I looked better with my hair off my shoulders. I was nervous at first, but now I find it quite liberating."

"You must really love your sister to follow her advice so readily."

"I have three sisters. And yes, I do love them very much. As of yet I know no one equal to their wisdom, strength, and beauty. Their advice hasn't let me down yet."

"Three sisters, and you are the youngest I suppose?" She nodded to him with another practiced smile. "The fourth sister... The fourth..." He stumbled on the next word.

"Princess," She finished for him. "You catch on rather slowly. Is it much farther? My ankle is really throbbing now." The poor lady was practically hopping on her good foot. She was also having trouble masking her pain with a smile.

"Not much, just around this corner." They came upon a thick wooden door with a small sign nailed to it that read:

Knock first. Objects may explode.

"Explode? Just where have you taken me?" She looked at the prince in complete dismay.

"That sign is new," he mumbled to himself. He turned to the lady and smiled, "Not to worry – I'm sure you won't explode..." He knocked loudly; no answer. He knocked again; No answer. The prince then started knocking rapidly on the door like a woodpecker determined to get a speck of grub. They finally heard the sound of padlocks turning, gears clapping, and hinges squeaking. Out peeked an older man with silver hair poking out from under his night cap. His small eyes squinted. His face turned from alarmed to annoyance as soon as he saw the prince. He opened the door wider and turned back to his room.

"Sire, I don't mind your visits but I actually have to get up in the morning. Not everyone has the same freedom to sleep as late as you can."

He hadn't looked up once as he set up a seat for the prince. Then, he filled up a pot of water to hang over the small fire in the hearth. This looked to be a rather routine visit for the old man.

"You haven't turned me away yet." The prince spoke with a charming smile.

"Right, right well… It's hard to say no when you have…" The old man looked up and caught his first view of the woman in the room. "Goodness!" The man cursed as he leaped for his robe. "And who might this young lady be?"

"This is, err, um… a visitor to the palace." The prince found it hard to introduce her formally as a princess. She said she was a princess and he had nothing but her appearance to contradict her. That didn't mean the prince believed her.

"I am known as the Fourth Princess, but you can call me Four." She held out her hand to the old man. He quickly took in her apparel with one glance. Then his eyes abruptly flicked back to her necklace, where he studied it for an extensive moment. Finally, he looked up into her deep brown eyes with a genuine smile.

"Oh my dear, welcome to our castle." The man took her hand in his and bowed formally to her. "I am Doctor Kendall Krouss, the fool, but everyone just calls me Fool."

Chapter

"How terrible! I will not call you that!" The princess objected.

"No, no," The prince chimed in. "That's what he is. This is our fool."

"You took me to your fool to treat my ankle? Have you lost your mind?"

The prince was surprised by her comment. For an instant she could see a glimmer of sadness in his eyes. He opened his mouth to respond, but the fool spoke instead.

"Oh my dear, do sit down." Fool helped her to a chair and propped her bad ankle on a table nearby. He couldn't help but allow another glance at the beautifully polished ring around her neck. "Please don't be confused. I am a doctor. Studied, practiced, and accomplished. I serve as the royal family's personal doctor *and*

I am also the fool. Apparently all my medical terms and phrases make people laugh in this place and now they won't let me go."

The princess was so confused. Here she was being treated by a fool who was actually a doctor, working for a prince, who acted like a fool when a princess knocked on his door. She allowed herself a small chuckle.

"See what I mean?" Fool said with a smile. He examined her ankle by poking and feeling around for any abnormalities. "You're very lucky it's only a sprain. I will need to wrap it and you must stay off it for a while. You will also need to elevate it to help bring down the swelling."

"How long is a while?" Asked the prince eagerly.

"A few weeks. A month to be safe."

"A month!? Oh no. That will not do! She can't stay here for a month."

"Well you can't send her away in a state like this. She could be permanently hurt!" Fool answered back.

"Where will she stay? No one stays here without Mother knowing. And when she sees her…" He gasped and threw up his hands, "That is not a meeting I want happening!"

"Excuse me," The princess had been allowing them to have their conversation and had grown tired of being overlooked. "I would love to meet the queen. I'm sure we will get along just fine, at least, long enough for me to get better."

"Oh no, you don't understand…" The prince started in a near panic. The fool interrupted him and sat him down so he could relax.

"My dear, don't take it personally." Fool started. "The queen is a very particular person. She enjoys her routine. The same things day after day. No surprises, no unexpected troubles. If she wants a change, it is by her order alone. People don't 'drop by', they are invited. The queen's life is scheduled to the minute and is a wreck when it is not followed directly. There is not much room for excitement and unpredictability. If she were to learn you were staying here, it would not fare well, even if it is an accident."

"So, what should I do?" The princess glanced at the prince who was stroking his chin in deep thought. She turned back to the Fool with pleading eyes.

The Fool coughed loudly. "You're Highness?"

The prince stood up with a small grin. "You can stay here in the Fool's room,"

"What?" Came the Fool's and the princess' answer in unison.

"Just a second ago you wanted me out as fast as possible!"

"Where am I going to stay if she is here? Just use a guest room for her or something!" Pleaded the Fool.

"How heartless do you think I am?" The Prince said acting sympathetic. "We wouldn't send you away with a twisted ankle. You need to rest up until you're better, no matter how long it takes."

"What?" They both blurted out in disbelief.

The Prince led the Fool to a corner before he spoke softly. "Fool, this castle is becoming gloomier by the day. You said it yourself, If she stays here, there might be some excitement for a change."

"A sprained ankle isn't excitement."

"It's better than the predictable monotone life that I've had to endure. If you even call that living. If she stays in your room, you can keep a better eye on her ankle, and Mom will never find out. You know she never walks these halls."

"This is a bad idea. People will talk. She will find out, then overreact in a terrible way!"

"No one 'talks' in this place. Everything will be fine!"

"Using an injured princess for your own personal entertainment is not 'fine'!"

THE FOURTH PRINCESS

"She's not a princess! And, I'm not using her. I'm helping! Be happy, I'm doing a nice thing!"

"But-!"

"No, it's settled…" He turned to the Princess and spoke up. "Make yourself comfortable, you will be my guest until you are well."

"Thank you," The princess said with a vague smile.

"Um, sire, there's still a small matter of… where do I sleep?!"

"The stables, of course."

"The stables!?"

"Yes, they're warm and dry-"

"You sleep in the stables then!!!"

"-And you won't draw attention out there. Now. See to her ankle!"

The Fool grumbled his way to the princess with some wrappings. As he wrapped her foot, he continued to mutter with an audible "Stables" and "It's cold".

"I can sleep in the stables." The Princess chimed in. "I've slept in many different stables. Yours will not trouble me."

"Oh my dear," The Fool responded. "I would never allow such a lovely woman to sleep in straw, especially in the state you're in." He faced the prince, shooting evil glares at him. "You, however, could use a month or so in the stables. Teach you some character!"

The prince simply laughed and dismissed the comment.

"Thank you, Doctor Fool, and thank you for your room too." The princess was more than grateful for his sacrifice.

He smiled at the woman, "For you, anything." He grabbed a pillow and blanket as he stormed out to the stables, shooting icy looks at the prince. "You are not my favorite person today."

"Okay, goodnight!" Said the prince with a smile as he slammed the door behind the fool, then smiled at his guest.

The princess gave him an unamused look. "Wow. You really have a way with your servants, don't you?"

"I do, actually." He answered cleaning the clutter off the bed. "The fool is my best friend in this place. He will be fine."

"If that's how you treat your best friend, I'd hate to see how you treat a stranger," She chimed sarcastically. "Oh! Excuse me, I already know."

He rubbed his hands on his neck trying to hide that it was flushing red. "Yes, well, I'm terribly sorry. You caught me at a bad time. No one comes here without business or an invitation, and business is always done in the morning. I was... off guard..."

"Well, I appreciate the apology."

"So," He poured her a cup of tea. "Will you tell me who you really are now?"

A smile spread across her lips as she held the tea warming her hands. "Still skeptical I see."

He shrugged. "Can you blame me?"

"Would you believe me if I told you I was a traveling philanthropist?"

"I'd sooner believe you were a traveling gypsy."

The princess smiled knowingly as she laughed softly to herself. "Alright. Let's use that then."

"Excuse me?"

"Well you don't believe the truth so... I'm a traveling gypsy looking for inspiration to create even better songs, and more captivating stories dripping with intrigue, drama and excitement. When I am done, I will return to my caravan to become the most well-known story teller of all time!" She took a sip of her tea with an amused smile while the prince stared at her flabbergasted.

"Okay, let it stay a secret then. At least may I know what to call you?"

THE FOURTH PRINCESS

"Well, since I know you won't believe me, I'll skip the mystery. I am Princess Josephine Helena Carmina, but as I told Doctor Fool my friends call me Four."

"Josephine it is," the Prince nodded to her.

"As you wish, your Highness," She mocked him for his obvious rejection toward her offer of friendship.

"Wendell. My name is Wendell."

"Wendell?" She looked doubtful.

"Yes. Is there a problem?"

"Not at all, you're Highness."

He grimaced as she called him *highness*, "So… What else can I fetch for you?"

"Honestly, it's been a long day. I should get some sleep.

"Right, of course." He didn't move from his seat as he kept staring, trying to puzzle her out.

"As in, *now*. I really should to go to sleep now."

"Oh, right!" He got up with a bit of disappointment on his face that did not escape the princess.

"Don't worry, I'll be here in the morning."

"I have to help with business in the morning… prince stuff. But, may I come by when it's over."

"Well, I don't think I'm going anywhere."

He laughed. "Alright. See you tomorrow. Goodnight, Josephine."

"Goodnight, you're Highness."

Chapter

The next morning, Josephine was woken by the fool rummaging through his things. He was trying hard not to disturb the princess, but failed miserably.

She yawned and stretched as she sat up to talk to him.

"You're up awfully early, Dr. Fool."

"What-?" He was startled by her voice. "Oh, good morning my dear. The queen likes me to be present when they go through morning business."

The princess blinked in surprise. "Do you help with the affairs too?"

"I help make the business not so dreary for the queen. She doesn't enjoy the daily gruel, so I liven it up for her."

"Seems a bit distracting, Doctor."

"Well," His voice was hushed and intent. "That is kind of the idea. If she's distracted, Prince Wendell is able to handle each matter without her noticing."

"Doesn't she run this country – as the queen?"

"Yes and no… She's not very good at it. So, the prince has been helping as best he can, without her knowledge."

"You mean the same halfwit who graciously let me in last night?"

Fool chuckled, "The very same! Honestly, you caught him at his worst. He is a good man and smart as a whip. He just doesn't get to spend much time around people." She nodded but didn't entirely believe the Fool. "Why don't you come along with me? You won't even be noticed. Then, you can see us in action."

"Spend my morning watching how the two of you manage the kingdom, and the queen, together?"

Fool shrugged and looked a bit embarrassed for asking.

She smiled. "Sounds delightful!"

He lead her down hidden hallways and behind tapestries that servants would usually keep to.

"I see the queen enjoys her servants out of sight?"

"For the most part." A glint came to his eye, "It also means more hiding places." They came to a large drape of deep blue velvet. A sliver of light sliced through the dark as Fool peeked behind it. "Here we are my dear. The Royal Throne Room. Have a look, it's still rather early."

Josephine stepped out into an amazing room. The white marble floor soaked in the sunlight, giving the room an omnipotent glow. The gold in-lay around the tiles and stairs twinkled like stars in the night sky, adding to the brilliance. Ahead of her was a rounded stairway that led to a platform with two golden thrones covered in ornate scrollwork. They were padded with the same deep blue velvet from the drapes. Off to the side were several oversized cushions and pillows of gold and blue fabrics. They were piled halfway up the stairs to the side of the thrones.

"How many cushions do they need, doctor?"

"Oh, those are for the prince. You see..." Before he could explain, they heard voices heading towards them. "Back!" He whispered in a hurried hiss. He lead her behind the drape and over to a grate, where she had a clear view of the room through the metal. "You can spy us from here. I'll come get you when it's over." He turned to enter the throne room once again only this time he entered while performing a few haphazard cartwheels and summersaults.

Josephine chuckled, "He really is a bad fool..." She whispered to herself.

The queen sauntered into the room dripping with grace and elegance. Following close behind was the prince, who looked as if he hadn't slept a wink last night. As the queen eased into her throne, the prince carelessly, flopped down onto the pile of cushions on the stairway. The queen motioned to a servant who had appeared at the bottom of the stairs.

The servant announced to the room, "Old Business."

Another servant holding a scroll appeared and bowed low to the queen. He began to read off a list of concerns or petitions that had been put off from their last meeting.

Josephine could hardly believe what she was seeing. The queen was staring blankly at the fool, lost in thought. Fool had started to juggle, only to drop several of the objects during each trick. He was doing a miserable job, but the princess laughed softly anyways. As the servant continued to read off the old business, she could hear the prince muttering in between readings. This was followed by a small nod of the head while the servant scribbled a note or two.

"Could he really be running the kingdom this way?" The princess whispered to herself.

Eventually, the servant rolled up his scroll and bowed deeply. That seemed to pull the queen out of her trance long enough to motion to her announcer.

"New Business," he called out.

Everyone seemed to follow the same roles as they had done for old business, only the queen would chime in with phrases such as:

"Must we discuss this today?"

"How much longer must we hear this?"

"This is giving me a headache…"

Interestingly though, when "Messages from Yesterday" was announced, the queen was fully attentive and replied to every note distinctly.

"Mother," Wendell spoke up. "Are we planning something here at the castle?"

"My dear boy, why do you ask?" She asked in an innocent tone.

"I can't help but notice we received several messages. Many of them saying 'We would be honored to attend!' Usually that means something's going on."

"Oh, my son…" She cooed in a patronizing voice. "Do not worry. No one is coming to see you. I am simply meeting with a few ladies – women's business."

Still looking concerned, the prince nodded to her. "Just keep me informed when they arrive, so I know not to get in the way."

"Of course, sweetheart!" The queen smiled.

Without much warning, morning business was over. It wasn't because the servant was finished reading, but because the queen simply stood up to leave the room announcing it was time for her to adjourn to the gardens. The princess assumed whatever wasn't covered would become tomorrows 'old business' and the process would begin again. She was grateful when the room had cleared and Fool waived her out of hiding. The prince, surprised again, stumbled to his feet from his cushions as he saw the princess limp into the room.

"Please, there's no need to get up," She smiled warmly at him.

"How long have you been here!?" Demanded the prince. His careless, carefree attitude that he had donned for morning business was clearly a façade. His stance and tone intimidated the Josephine for an instant.

She drew in her courage and spoke just as prominently, "I saw it all. Dr. Fool invited me to listen in."

"You did what?!" His hands clinched onto the Fool's collar, pulling him close.

"I wanted her to see the better side of you instead of the nervous, oaf you acted like last night!"

The fool had a way of telling someone the hard truth at exactly the right moment; when they actually listened.

The prince's face softened, he took a deep breath and let go of the fool. He turned to the princess. "And what have you learned?"

"Quite a bit. But, why not get rid of the secrets, and ask your mother turn the kingdom over to you?"

The prince and Fool burst into laughter.

"I have asked her," The prince started. "Many times in fact. She doesn't feel I'm ready to handle an entire kingdom on my own."

"But, you already are… handling things I mean. You're not doing a bad job of it either."

"Thank you – but she doesn't see it that way."

"Perhaps if you weren't so mysterious about ruling the kingdom, she will see things your way?"

"All I know is every time I speak up for business or stop helping entirely things go poorly for the kingdom. I can't allow that to happen, so we stick with what works."

THE FOURTH PRINCESS

"I understand," Josephine said with all the sympathy she had.

"Do you?" Wendell asked in disbelief.

"Of course I do. You're torn between your duties to your kingdom and your own personal desires. Many people struggle with this. All you need to do is find your balance… or so I've been told. It's not always easy to do. The problem is, no matter what we choose, we generally end up wrestling with the decision for the rest of our lives."

"You speak as if you've had this struggle," Wendell mocked.

"I struggle with it every day!" She retorted with a dignified glare. "A normal princess studies at home and waits patiently for her prince to come. In the end, she is supposed to live happily ever after because that's how things are done. Princesses don't travel from place to place working with common…" She cut herself off and took a deep breath calming herself. She looked up at him with a masking smile, "My parents want me home studying, so I can become an exemplary queen. That way, *any* prince who comes along would be honored to ask for my hand in marriage. I, on the other hand, want to be free of the palace. There are things I can learn from helping people that I would never have learned from study alone. I want to see things and learn about them for myself. And, hopefully, learn how I fit in this world."

The Prince breathed an amazed "Wow, you're good. I almost believe you." Then he smiled and continued "It's a good thing you're not a princess or you'd have a hurricane of a struggle on your mind."

"I am a princess, your highness!" She snapped

"No. I don't think so. But your story was very entertaining."

"Lying to yourself over and over will never make it true."

"Indeed!" He agreed with a pointed look at her.

"Okay," Fool interrupted as Josephine opened her mouth to argue. "I think it's time we put that foot up again. Come, let's get you back to bed. Why don't you tell us of your travels, Josephine?" The older man spoke while directing a sharp look at the younger man. This was his way of offering the prince a chance to restrain his attitude and be polite again. "I'm sure that's a topic we would love to entertain."

Prince Wendell composed himself under the penetrating glare of his fool. "Yes, that would be a lovely conversation over brunch. Fool, will you please have a tray of food made up and bring it to your room when it's ready?"

The fool smiled at the prince, "Absolutely, your highness." He turned and headed towards the kitchen.

Prince Wendell offered his arm to Josephine, who took it gratefully. Josephine may have been upset with the prince, but the pain of her ankle was too great to refuse any offer of help. She decided to change the subject.

"I noticed the king wasn't at the meeting this morning. Is he well?"

The prince breathed loudly. It was his turn to give her a blank smile that covered up a torrent of emotion.

"My father has been sick for a while. He spends most of his time in his chambers."

"I'm sorry. Is that why you spend most of your time with the fool?"

"I spend most of my time with Fool because he is my best friend. He is always there for me, no matter the reason."

"That does sound like a good friend. Perhaps you shouldn't get angry with him so easily."

Prince Wendell smiled. "Oh, I assure you, he gets just as angry with me. We look out for each other."

Josephine allowed a small laugh. "The prince and the fool looking out for each other. That's an amusing friendship."

Prince Wendell grew defensive in a second. "I'll have you know, the fool is one of the smartest men I have ever met. He has taught me invaluable lessons that no one else has ever taken the time to share. He is highly educated, and uses his knowledge to pioneer new ideas that could change the world. Anyone who sees him as a simple fool is only fooling themselves."

Josephine blushed from embarrassment. "Forgive me. I didn't mean to disrespect you or the fool. I just find your relationship… unexpected is all."

"And you find the unexpected amusing?" the prince studied her carefully.

"I delight in the unexpected. I find it refreshing when anything challenges the predictability of life in general. The world would be a very dull place without some surprises to help mix things up. Wouldn't you agree?"

"Josephine, I believe we have finally found something we can agree on."

He gave her a small bow as he opened the door to the fool's room for her. Down the hall they could see Fool hurrying towards them with a silver platter piled high with delicious fruits and pastries. Once in the room, Josephine settled back onto the bed as the prince piled up pillows under her foot to keep it elevated. A chair and table were placed next to the so called princess, so the young adults could talk privately while munching on some brunch. Fool grabbed a few items and retreated to his desk. He silently nibbled his scraps while pawing over some old books and leafs of paper filled with notes he had taken down. The older man left the two youngsters to their conversation.

"Where have you visited?" Wendell asked; genuinely interested for the first time in what she was going to say.

"So many places it's hard to remember them all in one sitting. When you have been traveling for many years, things like boundaries seem trivial. Every kingdom has their own unique flair for things, naturally. But, at the heart of it, they all have the same problems to work through, the same people working hard to scrape up a living, and the same simple joys that make the daily grind worthwhile. It's hard to know when I crossed from one kingdom to another.

Wendell smiled at her comment. He was quite familiar with the nearby kingdoms and their unique flair, as Josephine mentioned. Then he wondered about his own kingdom, and what was unique about them. "You must remember a few favorites though."

This earned him a warm, if not fond, smile. "Yes, there are a few." The princess went on to discuss different kingdoms, describing each by the people who lived there and what they loved to do. She told the prince about different families she had stayed with and helped with each families' trade. She taught one set of farmers a better way to water the crops using less energy. Another person she stayed with, a blacksmith, she had helped develop a way to keep the furnaces hot with less fuel. There were many more stories she told. In each one Josephine always spoke of how she worked with someone and what they were able to accomplish together. When she came to tell of how she assisted with the birth of a woman's beautiful child, she had trouble holding back emotional tears.

As she told each story she could see the prince become more and more interested. Doubt slowly melted away from his eyes; finally, he was starting to look at her as an equal. At times she thought he looked like an eager little boy listening to a story played out by a performer. That made her smile. He started to ask questions and only seemed more impressed when she was able to answer each one easily with more details. He started to add his own comments to her stories. Before long, they were both enjoying a pleasant conversation. Brunch slowly blended into dinner as the hours seemed to fly by through story telling.

"But the most outrageous thing was the time I stopped a war," She mentioned while munching on a treat from the dinner tray. Time had disappeared so quickly that no one took the opportunity to notice.

"Wait! I have been with you this whole time and followed your every word… but I find it hard to believe that you singlehandedly stopped a war." He laughed awkwardly, then relaxed when she laughed too.

"I still find it hard to believe myself, and I was there! But, it happened. They were fighting over land. I suppose that is nothing new when it comes to war. One kingdom, needed more land for farming. They were importing more than they should which led to overspending."

He nodded in agreement but kept a tight stare on her, waiting for her gallant deed.

"I had the chance to look over their maps and found a large chunk of unused land that was already theirs."

"Why weren't they using it?"

"Well, their maps were outdated. It showed the area to be desolate, a place where nothing could survive. Lucky for me, I came into their kingdom through that land and saw it was a beautiful place with green fields and flowing streams. The wildlife had reclaimed the area and actually made it better. I took the king to see the space for himself. He was so surprised that he immediately ordered two explorers to re-chart his entire kingdom. They had their land and no blood was spilled.

"But what about the neighboring kingdom? Were they angry when the king cut his spending?"

"I convinced the king that less money is better than no money from debt. "I also told him how other kingdoms store their surpluses; saving it for years when the crops are not as promising. He was so excited by the idea, his anger disappeared."

The prince leaned back in his chair astounded. "Just like that, no more war?"

"I assume so. There was a huge festival for the next few days thrown by both kings. I hope their friendship lasts a long time."

Wendell chuckled and lifted his glass to her. "I must say, you do have a way with people. Here's to you and your extraordinary experiences."

"Thank you," she smiled. "I look forward to hearing about you and your kingdom. I'm sure you have wondrous stories to tell, as well."

Wendell's smile fell from his face as his eyes grew to the size of saucers. "Me? You expect *me* to impress the famous Fourth Princess? After everything you just said?"

"My goodness, no… I expect you to be yourself and tell me what your kingdom is like."

"How can this kingdom, or myself… compare to all the places you have been to? And the people…"

"Every place is different." Josephine interrupted. "And each person is unique. There is no 'best' or 'worst'. There is simply… you. Relax, you are already leaving a memorable impression."

"Ah, that's comforting. Well, I should allow you to rest then, since it is late. May I come see you tomorrow?"

"You may. I enjoy this nicer version of you.'

"Right," Wendell smiled as he blushed. Then, to avoid any further embarrassment, he quickly dismissed himself.

"Goodnight!" Josephine said as she watched the prince fumble to the door.

"Oh, yes. Indeed. Goodnight." He flinched slightly as he closed the door a little too roughly causing it to slam shut.

"It would seem you've made an impression on the prince," The fool commented as if he were talking about the weather. Josephine didn't notice as the old man stole a few glances at her while he pretended to study his notes. He stifled any further remark when he noticed a small blush on her cheeks when she tried not to smile. It was a perfect match to Prince Wendell's awkward smile a moment ago. As for the fool, it took every bit of energy not to laugh at the two of them.

Chapter

For someone who preferred to be outside of a stuffy castle, actively working on something, the days seemed to crawl by for Josephine. She was thrilled to pieces when she was told her horse was found. She tried to sneak off to the stables to take care of him, or perhaps risk a ride. But, the fool put his foot down telling her that a walk or even a ride would only make her ankle worse. Thanks to the doctor's order, the fool's little room continued to be her entire world. Prince Wendell visited often to give her company; however, there were duties even he couldn't avoid. Whenever boredom crept in, the princess would read the books from the fools' library. As she read, she learned all sorts of things about healing herbs and foods, she even took down a few notes to tuck away for future reference. One day she was so bored that she chose to clean his room. Normally, Josephine avoided cleaning at all costs. However; when you are stuck in a room for so long, and forced to see piles of things itching to topple on top of you… cleaning doesn't seem like a bad idea.

Josephine started by collecting up all the dirty clothes first, followed by beating the dust from the drapes, cleaning dishes, dusting shelves, and straightening up the library last. She took particular care to avoid disturbing the desk covered with open books and cluttered notes sprawled across it. She assumed everything on his desk was exactly where Dr. Fool wanted it. Josephine was able to clear away a few empty ink bottles, when one particular piece of paper happened to catch her eye. Scrawled all over the page were silly thoughts like:

"Wendell loves Joe"

"Joe loves Wendy"

"His Highness and Josephine"

Josephine allowed an amused laugh then casually tossed the page directly into the fire.

"This doctor is a horrible fool!" She laughed as she sat down in a chair for a quick rest and to give her aching ankle a break. The princess had no idea she had drifted off to sleep until she was shaken awake by the fool.

"What have you done?! Where is it all? Who gave you permission?"

"What…? Where is what? Permission for what?"

"To clean this room!" The fool howled.

Josephine was so shaken she actually felt guilty. "I'm sorry doctor… I thought you would appreciate—"

"My clothes washed, dishes sent away and the dust gone?!" Josephine wanted to respond but by now he was far too upset. "And I suppose you rifled through my research too!"

"No!" She shouted, finding her confidence again. "I only cleared away the empty things. I didn't touch any books or papers."

The Fool was foraging around his desk muttering to himself. He looked up with an icy glare. "Liar!"

"Excuse me?" The princess was shocked.

"What did you take?" He insisted.

"Nothing! I don't know what you're talking about!"

He drew closer to her so they were almost nose to nose. "Liar, I can tell you're lying. You are terrible at it!"

"But I didn't… hold on!" His words rattled her mind. "What exactly have I lied about?"

His eyes narrowed and voice calmed to a solemn tone. "Absolutely nothing… Until now."

The princess blinked in surprise. "You believe me? You actually believe I am a princess?"

'Well, of course I do."

"No one believes me!" the princess declared still stunned.

"My dear, I believe you. Now, what did you take?" He was still very serious with her.

"I may have cleared away a page."

"One page. I hope it wasn't the page with my very special notes?"

"Very special…?"

"You know the one." He encouraged.

"Um, yes? I didn't see anything special though!"

"Where is it?"

"In the fire, doctor, I'm so sorry! It looked like a joke!"

"Did you read any more of my notes?"

"No! I swear. Just the one right on top!" She promised.

His voice turned happy again as he sat down next to her. "Well you should have. It's one of the most exciting things you could ever hope to learn."

Josephine was a wash of confusion. She had no idea how to respond to the fool. "Am I missing something?" She asked. "What about the document?"

"Oh, that's my decoy page. I leave it on my notes in just the right place, so I know when its been moved. Its only purpose is to help me know when someone's been snooping through my work."

She let out a tremendous sigh and finally caught up to the new conversation's subject. "Seems a bit too confusing for me. There are so many different combinations of powders and shells. Not to mention that one false move could result in a premature explosion."

"You know how to follow a recipe?" The fool asked Josephine, and she nodded slowly. "Then you can do this easily. Simply use the right ingredients and follow the directions exactly."

"Aright, now I'm interested." She joined the fool at his desk to look at what he was showing her.

"When you mix, make sure to mix carefully and slowly. Otherwise you may lose those eyebrows, or your beautiful bangs."

Before she could learn any more of the Fool's secret project, the door banged open. Josephine and the Fool jumped at the sound and looked up just in time to see the prince flop down in a chair as the door slammed shut from its recoil. The fool motioned to Josephine to go talk to him. Not wanting to walk straight into Wendell's bad mood, she glared at the fool and shook her head. Fool nudged her around the desk encouraging her to say something. With a silent sigh, she sat on a nearby stool; close enough to talk but just far enough to duck in case any objects became airborne.

"Well you look..." She searched around in her head for something nice to start with but couldn't find anything. His clothes were rumpled, his hair was a mess, and he had bags under his eyes. Prince Wendell's face looked sunken, hollow, with a combination of rage and fear painted there.

The princess took a deep breath, but instead of saying something profound and uplifting, she blurted out, "You look awful!" She rolled her eyes at her pitiful attempt at sensitivity.

"Well it's hard to look dashing every moment of the day."

Her eyes widened a little as she nodded to the prince. She tried everything she could to keep a blank unreadable face, but she couldn't stop the small smirk curving her lips. She was relieved to see a similar smile soften his face and his muscles relax.

"Now then, shall I start commenting on your clothes as well or may we skip the small talk? Personally, I would rather just know what on earth is going on."

Wendell took a deep breath as he rubbed his hands over his face. "Mother is setting me up again."

The fool dropped his work. "Again? Are you certain?"

"Undoubtedly. I caught her making ballroom arrangements with some of the staff."

"Sorry, what does that mean?" Josephine asked.

"My mother, the queen, wants me to get married."

The princess's eyebrows shot up. Her mouth hung open as she chose her next words carefully.

"Well, marriage can be a frightful thing."

"Yes, it can be! Especially when you don't have a say in the matter," the prince muttered in agreement.

Josephine looked at the fool for some help filling in the gaps. "I thought the prince was allowed to choose his wife. At least, where I'm from they do. I'm not seeing the problem."

Fool started, "Well, as you have learned, we have a very… particular… queen. So particular that she selects and arranges meetings with princesses who are later matched with Wendell to determine the best fit."

"And she hasn't found one yet?"

Wendell began pacing back and forth, burning off a little of his rage. "She has found plenty of princesses! The problem is I despise all of them!" he fumed. "She cares nothing for what I want; and she ends up picking a glowing, pristine, miniature of her!"

"So tell her what you're looking for this time," Josephine suggested.

"Right! What an easy fix. Why didn't I think of that before?" The sarcasm flew out of Wendell's mouth and slapped his guest in the face. She recoiled.

"Well you must have done something to get out of it before now. You did mention this wasn't the first time she's tried to marry you off."

The prince sighed as he fell back into the chair. "I think I've just been lucky before. I don't know what else I can do to avoid this."

"Well, I wouldn't want to avoid it," She responded softly.

"Excuse me?"

Josephine couldn't believe she had said those words out loud! What was even more terrifying was the prince heard it all very clearly. She looked up to meet his skeptical eyes trying not to trip over her thoughts and smoothly added to the words she had already spoken. "Your mother is expecting you to avoid it at all costs. She is probably waiting you out until you finally give in, much like you're about to do now. I think it would be better if you changed things up. You say your mother likes things to be predictable and in order, right? Then, you need to throw a wild card into her game and eliminate the secrecy all together. Who knows, you might actually like the outcome of these meetings." She was proud of herself for not stuttering over her last minute correction. The one thing she didn't want was to be embarrassed in front of the prince, especially by her own carelessness.

"I highly doubt I'll enjoy any outcome she may come to." Wendell scoffed, then thought for a moment. "You are right about the rest. If anything, I can find a flaw or a weakness in her plan and end it all together."

"I couldn't agree more." The princess was proud, of Wendell. The prince was taking control of his own life, or at least he was thinking about it. He had not moved from his chair, consumed by his own thoughts. She snapped her fingers in front of his face.

"Prince Wendell," she shouted.

"Yes!" He jumped.

"Don't you have someplace you should be getting to? Other than here?" She hinted with a gesture at the door. He continued to stare at her blankly. "Perhaps telling your mother you want to participate in her plans?"

"Oh, yes, you're right." He got up to leave.

The door slammed after him leaving behind a slightly awkward silence.

Fool turned towards the princess. "Are you alright, my dear?"

Josephine wheeled around and looked at him. "Of course I'm alright, why wouldn't I be?"

"I don't know, for a moment there it looked like you really wanted to 'participate' as well," he grinned.

"A competition to win over the queen to marry the prince? Certainly not. It's all a load of nonsense." She hadn't noticed she was wringing a blanket in her hands while staring at the door.

The fool raised his eyebrow at her as he returned to his work. In the softest voice only he would hear, he whispered one word with a smile. "Liar."

Chapter

The princess had found a new hobby to pass the time. She poured over Fool's notes and recipes learning as much as she could. She read more about potions and the new concoctions he had invented. She learned about burn time, burn patterns, color, timing, layering, wrapping… everything a small piece of an elaborate puzzle. Josephine enjoyed the temporary apprenticeship she seemed to have developed with the fool, and looked forward to their many experiments.

However, as exciting as it may be, she missed having the prince around. Ever since Wendell realized his mother was conspiring to have him married, he had been spending more time with her and her… guests. Of course, that was entirely Josephine's fault. It had been her own advice to get close to observe and possibly reject potential matches. Chatting in Fool's room used to be a primary part of his everyday routine. Now, she was lucky if he came by every other day. Even then, the conversations were usually about the dismal princesses he had to endure.

Josephine couldn't help but wonder what the 'next girl' he would be presented to would be like. The first had been downright rude to him. Every time she spoke it had been directed at his mother, not Wendell. He would try to talk to her only to be ignored. Apparently the reason for that, he found out later, was she thought him to be a servant; her personal valet when she became queen. Josephine felt terrible when she laughed at his story. He didn't mind and continued to joke around speculating what his life would be like with her. In no time, the two of them were in stiches as they imagined him posing as a footstool for the princess, while she mindlessly asked "Where has my husband gone?"

The next was completely oblivious to just about everything. Even the queen admitted to it, but she was breathtakingly beautiful. When asked what she thought of the prince her answer was, "He's nice." Of course, this was the same answer she gave about the ride in, the gardens, the stables, the servants, and just about anything else.

"At least you know she'll be a *nice* queen," Josephine had commented, trying to find a bright side.

Wendell simply rolled his eyes.

As dreadful as those princesses were, they couldn't deny that other candidates the Queen selected were actually quite lovely. Whenever Josephine admitted to the prince that the princess in one of his stories sounded like a good match, she would often hear him grumble the words Perfect Porcelain Dolls. When Josephine finally found the courage to ask what that meant, all she got was, "They don't want to be scratched." She pretended that she understood and left it at that. Josephine had a feeling that if she poked deeper, it would make his foul mood even worse.

Then there was Olivia. Wow. This woman was all charm and grace along with intellect and responsibility. The queen loved her immediately. Even the prince wasn't deterred by her. It would seem his mother wasn't entirely oblivious to his own wants and desires. Until, that is, she left the room leaving Prince Wendell and Princess Olivia alone. Her entire countenance changed. There was nothing about the castle she liked. She made comments on what changes needed to be made. The princess was entirely rude to the servants, and at lunch had a complaint about everything she tasted. She even zeroed in on the prince; barking orders like 'be quiet' and 'fix that slouch.' He finally had enough when she commented on his height.

"Princess Olivia, you are being entirely rude! And I'm not sure I can endure much more!" The prince stated.

"Frankly," the princess answered with a shrug. "I don't care. Clearly your mother is in charge around here. In case you haven't noticed, *she* loves me. This kingdom will be my crowning glory. And you? You are too flimsy and weak to stop it."

Josephine's jaw dropped and hung open when the prince told her the story. "Oh, she has got to go!"

"How? My mother adores her, and she doesn't believe anything I say!"

That was the moment when Josephine started to hate these stories. Every last one. She hated how the princesses were acting. She would never have gotten away with such attitude back home. She hated how the prince's mood seemed to sour more and more each day. Even more, she hated how his mother was wearing on him. It was beginning to look like he was ready to concede and allow the queen to marry him to one of these, so called… *princesses*. The whole thing disgusted her.

If I had a chance to meet the queen, she thought, *I would tell her everything she's missing! I would show her how smart and responsible her son is. She has to be told how Wendell is the one making the decisions around here, and the people in kingdom are happy because of it! I would tell her how ridiculous it is to force marriage onto her son knowing how miserable he would be with any of them. I would show her how he has proven over and over again how capable he is. I would help her to see him the way I do, and show him all that I love about him!*

"Are you alright, my dear?" The fool's voice sounded distant, even though he was right in front of her, unwrapping her ankle.

"I'm sorry?" Josephine asked.

"You went really still suddenly and your face focused – like stone. I was worried."

"Oh…" She took the bandages from him. "Yes, I must have been lost in thought for a moment."

"Thinking about Wendell, are you?"

Her eyes snapped up and narrowed on the fool. The man didn't even flinch.

"Me too, I'm worried about him. He's not acting like himself lately."

"I have only known him a short time. Who am I to know how he normally acts?" Each word sliced through the air as if hunting for blood.

Just then the prince entered the room heading straight to the fireplace to pour himself a cup of tea.

"Maybe you should just ask," whispered the fool as he motioned towards the disgruntled looking young man. Then he promptly settled behind his desk and buried himself into his notes.

Chapter

Josephine joined the prince by the fireplace as she settled into one of the stuffed chairs. Wendell gave Josephine an informal nod, poured her a mug of tea and found a seat as well. "Good evening." His voice was weighed down with fatigue. Josephine blew across her mug to cool her tea. At least, that's what she wanted him to think. She was trying to steady her emotions, so she would have a clear mind for the prince.

"Good evening," Josephine nodded as she sipped her tea.

"How is your ankle coming along?" he routinely asked.

"Oh, very well. I can move it much easier now."

"Excellent!" He caught himself. "Excellent, meaning that you are feeling better."

"Of course." She nodded. "And how are you feeling?"

The prince peered into his cup for was a moment. "Pretty spent. It was a long day with much to do."

"I can imagine. Running a kingdom is hard work." She relaxed a little when he didn't mention any of the princesses of the day.

"Running the kingdom and wife searching."

"And there it is," She mumbled. Her body tensed again as she set down her tea.

The prince wasn't distracted by her comment. "You should have seen the line up my mother had for me. About halfway through the day my brain simply shut off due to boredom. I couldn't tell you half the things I said to them…"

"Could we, please, not talk about this?"

"What?"

"I'm sorry. I'm just tired. That's all."

"Tired? You? But you always want to talk with me."

"Yes well… I do love our conversations."

"But you're tired?"

She sighed, "I'm tired of hearing story after story about these… *fools*!" she turned, "No offense, Doctor."

"None taken." Fool murmured without looking up, but still clearly attentive to the conversation.

"Fools? Well, I admit a few are out there. But some are…"

"You included!" she interrupted.

The prince locked eyes in a glare with her. He was completely attentive to her now. "Me? How so?"

"Exactly when did you decide you were going to allow your mother to control your life?"

"I have never!"

"You're playing along quite easily then."

"Hey! I recall you were the one telling me to play along with her plans."

"And I recall you wanting to debunk this whole scheme before it even started. And yet here we are, down to the headliners with no end in sight!"

"I need to play along to convince my mother to include me in decisions. It's all an act."

"And how long does this play out? When you're old and married to one of those girls? Will it still be an act?"

"Come on, it won't go that far."

"It already has—you are allowing this scheme to happen right under your nose."

"I have to, otherwise she will catch on that I'm there to ruin her plans."

"But your lack of action tells her you are accepting whatever she does! Every day you tell me about each princess and the events of your meetings, which usually consists of your mother interviewing and you sitting back, watching. You tell me stories of these atrocious women and then ask me my opinion, as if I were a part in all of this."

"I was trying to include you so I could have someone to be honest with."

"You want honesty? Instead of asking me which princess I would choose, why haven't you asked me how to get rid of them?"

"Yeah? And you are an expert on that?"

"Well, I wouldn't call me an expert, but I have had to shake off some potential lovers."

"Oh, is that how you came by that handsome ring you hang around your neck? A token from one of your former lovers?"

Josephine was disgusted by his attitude, "My mother gave me this ring."

Prince Wendell rolled his eyes at her answer.

"Whatever you say." His response dripped with sarcasm which made Josephine's blood start to boil. "But, you can't just shake off potential royal engagements."

"Yes you can, I've done it. Every one of my sisters have done it!"

"Alright, now I KNOW you're lying because no princess in her right mind would turn down the chance to be married."

"Just because you haven't seen it done, doesn't mean it never happens."

"Not with royalty! You, and obviously your sisters, are not princesses."

"All my sisters are queens, and I am most assuredly a princess."

Prince Wendell slammed his mug down in a spat of rage.

"I thought we were being completely honest?" His eyes drilled into hers unwilling to accept any new stories today.

"Fine, let's have some more honesty. Why haven't you told your mother or any of these girls that you are not ready to be married? Why are you so willing to let you mother dominate your life while you are the one who knows what you want? The TRUTH, your highness, can you honestly tell me that you have done your best to end all this?"

Wendell stared at her, unable to speak. She waited, as patiently as she could, but an answer never came.

"So it's true. You have committed yourself to the idea that you *will* marry one of these women. Never mind the complete and utter misery you'll endure by being married to someone you care nothing about."

"That's what a royal marriage is about! Love is a luxury that royalty can never afford. I need to marry someone who can ensure the prosperity of my kingdom. They deserve someone they can accept and *they* will love as their queen."

"Now you sound like your mother!" The fool chimed in as if he was commenting on a play that was unfolding in front of him.

Prince Wendell and Josephine both shot steely looks at the Fool who had clearly made it known he was intentionally eavesdropping. But the prince is who spoke.

"I don't need your opinion, Fool!" The fool jumped once he realized he had spoken his comment far too loud, and decided to keep the rest of his thoughts in his head… for now.

"You think they deserve someone bereft of emotion? Someone that not even their king can love? You think they are going to tolerate anyone who is selfish, rude, ignorant… or any qualities these women have shown you?"

"I have yet to meet a princess who isn't like that to some degree."

"Seriously!? Those are the qualities you associate with a princess? I suppose I should consider myself lucky that you don't recognize me as one."

"You are NOT a princess."

"And just as well. If I was, you would throw me in with a lot of them and never give me another thought."

"But you are not a princess!"

Fire sparked in Josephine's eyes as she stood up. Her voice was calm and controlled yet it boomed with authority and contempt. "I am Princess Josephine Helena Carmina, Fourth daughter of Ronald, guardian of his everlasting wisdom and prosperity over the kingdom of Ebren. And I, as your friend, am obligated to tell you; you're making a terrible mistake!"

She grabbed her coat and left the room with a slam of the door.

Chapter  10

P rince Wendell looked around the room, all traces of her were gone in the blink of an eye. When they first met, he remembered Josephine telling him she traveled light. Likes to keep her things 'organized and within close reach' was what she said. His eyes rested on the fool who was doing his best to ignore the prince.

"Ha, can you believe her?" He was trying to understand exactly how his conversation started with *good evening* and ended with a shouting match.

"Actually, I do," the Fool said.

"And where could she have possibly stormed off to?" he considered his own question for a moment. "You don't think she would leave," his tone changed. "Do you?"

Fool looked up from his work and glared hard at the prince. The old man's raised eyebrow made Wendell feel small in the already miniscule room. A strange, new feeling washed over the prince. He had grown up alone in this castle with few friends to speak of. However, for the first time he felt lonely. In an instant he was on his feet racing down the hallways after her. Door after door blurred beside him as his eyes were fixed straight ahead, towards Josephine. He quickly caught up with her in the stables where she was preparing her horse for a journey.

"Josephine, stop!"

She stopped and turned towards Wendell, her eyes burning like ice. The prince faltered a bit. Anger was not something he had seen from her before and the intensity made him shudder. Despite the torrent of rage that boiled inside of her, Josephine managed to look calm and composed. There were so many things he could have said, so many ways to start.

Instead of starting with something profound and smooth he simply said, "I am a fool."

She stared at him, unimpressed.

He continued firm, but not angry. "I don't tell you things to upset you. You're the only one I want to talk to about all this. Right now my mind is so jumbled I'm not thinking straight. It's hard to know what to do, let alone say."

Josephine considered him for a while. She expected him to say more, but nothing else came. She was trying to decide if he was telling the truth or not. The confusion and hint of fear in his voice told her to relax just a little. Josephine took a deep breath, "Well, sometimes the best ideas come when you're not thinking. So I usually go somewhere that won't let me think."

"That makes… no sense."

She eyed him, not entirely ready to forgive him, "You only say that because you have never done it."

"So where do you suggest we go?"

"Have you ever been to town?" her eyes brightened as her lips hinted a genuine smile.

"I've ridden through it."

Her eyes rolled at him as she got on her horse. "Don't worry. I'll keep you in the shallows so you don't drown." She started a slow trot out away from the castle where she allowed her horse to meander a bit while the prince caught up.

Chapter

The tavern on the edge of town was simple and modest. A large strawberry field bursting with berries flowed behind it infecting the patrons inside with their sweet, delicious smell. Inside, tables with benches filled up the bulk of the room while a long bar ran along the back blocking off the door to the kitchen. Josephine and Wendell sat next to a fireplace off to one side of the main room. After a short while they ordered a few drinks and quietly kept to themselves while sipping them.

A tall young woman, who worked at the tavern, glided over to the couple and greeted them with a smile. "Hi! Is there anything you need?"

"No thanks, we won't be staying long." Said the prince.

It was unfortunate for him that Josephine said at the same time "Keep the drinks coming." She scowled at the prince daring him to counter her. "I'm sure we'll want to snack on a few things later though."

The maid smiled and winked at Josephine. "You got it. Any requests?"

"Just more of this will do." The prince mumbled as he nodded toward his mug.

"Surprise me!" Josephine said.

The girl giggled as she whirled away to the kitchens.

Josephine watched her go with a smile before turning to the prince. "You could at least try to enjoy yourself."

"I am enjoying myself… but would it be too much for them to wipe the tables down a bit more?" He asked with a raised eyebrow.

"It's added charm, for the ambiance?"

"Ambiance, what ambiance? As in the bored unamused faces of everyone here?"

"I don't know, it has potential for sure. The night is still young."

"Yeah… and soon this place will be full of drunkards. Maybe we should go now, before it gets more crowded." He huffed as he blew a bread crumb off the table then lounged back in his chair. "Where is that girl with the drinks anyways?" He muttered looking around, bored.

"I can see her at the table, over there." She spotted the golden haired beauty chuckling with a small group of young men. They looked familiar to Josephine and she turned her gaze towards the fire, to not appear rude by staring. She tried to remember why they were familiar.

Prince Wendell looked at Josephine and cocked his head to the side. "... Something bothering you with the fire? Coals too red? Flames too orange? Realizing your breath smells horrible?"

She immediately sat up with her hand covering her mouth. "My breath? Is it really that bad? Since when?"

The prince actually laughed a little at her, "No it's not. You're fine. I was just trying to get your attention." She shook her head at him.

"What is wrong with you? There are nicer ways to get my attention." She dropped her hand with great reluctance. Regardless of what he said, she would make sure to ask for a tray of mint leaves to chew on when the waitress came back. She offered a smile, "I was just thinking, is all. I recognize the group over there, but I can't quite place them yet."

They watched as the waitress danced from table to table serving plates of food, filling mugs, clearing scraps. All with a smile on her face and a playful word on her lips.

The waitress came back over to fill their glasses. "Sorry that took a bit. Are you ready for anything to eat? How's your evening going? Mine's peachy! Well… kind of… It's… yeah…" She glanced over her shoulder and flushed lightly as she looked back at Josephine and Wendell, hoping they hadn't noticed.

The prince raised his eyebrow again before looking at Josephine, amused. "Is there anything good to eat here?"

She didn't answer. Josephine looked up to see the girl peering over her shoulder again. She followed her gaze to find a young man sitting at the bar, hovering over a hot bowl. The look in his face was one of boredom, but the waitress's eyes dripped with longing.

Josephine cleared her throat to get the girl's attention.

"Sorry, what was the question?"

"A warm bowl of something sounds really good to me." Josephine casually mentioned. "That man at the bar, what does he have?"

The waitress turned again, anxious for another excuse to drink in his presence. "Hum… Just… Just a simple stew and bread," she said turning back to the couple. Would you like some? It's really good." Josephine saw their server's eyes wander back over her shoulder to the man at the bar with a soft, forgotten, puppy like sigh.

"Sure, why not?" the prince smiled. He was tempted to encourage her to go talk and interact with him, but thought better of it.

Just then a round, stump of a man hobbled over to the waitress while wiping his hands with a towel. He saw her standing still and staring off into what he presumed was nothing.

"Marie! Isn't there something better you can be doing with your time?"

"Of course!" she turned to Josephine and Wendell. "Two stews coming right up!" With a smile she disappeared again.

"I hope you are finding everything to your liking," he said nervously.

The prince looked up at him and smiled. "Yeah. I think everything is alright. Yet to try the food, but the drinks taste good. What say you, Josephine?"

Instead of answering, Josephine leaned toward the man, "Is it always like this?"

"Sorry?" The man rubbed the side of his head unsure of what to say.

"Your tavern, is it always this busy?"

"I'm not sure how many taverns you've been in my dear but 'busy' is not what I would call tonight. We used to be a thriving business, but now…" He trailed off looking embarrassed.

"What is it?" Wendell asked a little concerned.

"I don't mean to speak ill of the king. He is a great man and treats us very well. I just don't understand why he needs so many strawberries."

"Strawberries?" Josephine looked toward the prince for some kind of information. When his stone face revealed nothing, she turned back to the tavern owner. "What do strawberries have to do this?"

"For several years now, all the strawberries grown here are sent to the castle by order of the king. I think they are his favorite and they keep him happy, or something to that nature. I'm still unsure of it all."

Josephine shook her head, "I'm still not following. What does the king have to do with your business?"

The owner brightened up, "We used to make the most delicious strawberry pastries! Old family recipes that no one could outdo! Strawberry pies, strawberry tarts, cookies and bread, wine, you name it! People would come from all over the country for a sample of our treats. But now… well," He heaved a heavy sigh as he went back to work.

The prince watched him go and furrowed his brow, in thought.

"I remember now!" Josephine shouted while snapping her fingers.

The prince jumped in spite of himself. "What is it?"

"Korrin, that's where I know them from! The group over there, they're a traveling band. I saw them play in Korrin while I was a guest of the Lady Evangeline and Lord Abernathy. Oh they are amazing!"

"The Lord and Lady?"

"No, the musicians! They played all night long into to the morning for a ball that was being held. Such captivating, and brilliant music." She looked at their table and concentrated for a moment. "I wonder if they would be willing to play for us tonight."

"Good luck with that, they look quite content doing nothing at all."

The smell of stew paused their conversation as Marie appeared with bowls and a loaf of bread to share.

The prince contentedly started to eat. Then he looked back up at Josephine, "Anyways, concerning music, I don't think they'll be willing to play anything other than lazy picks on their instruments. I mean, look at their faces. They look like they'd rather be anywhere than here."

"I'm sorry, all I heard was 'Music, Play and Here." She ignored the prince's frustration as she concentrated on the musicians. "I bet I could get them to play." She whispered to herself. "I'm pretty sure I can. Yes, I know I can!"

Chapter 12

Prince Wendell rolled his eyes at Josephine. The musicians seemed to be chatting idly amongst one another, ignoring the rest of the tavern. Clearly, they had little to no interest in entertaining tonight. Instead of protesting the matter he allowed Josephine to entertain her own thoughts. He had learned by now when she put her energies toward something it was best just to stand aside and leave her to her schemes. It was a pastime of Josephine's that was now rubbing off on him. He found himself lost in his own thoughts trying to solve a newfound mystery. He couldn't understand why all the strawberries from the field were being sent to the castle.

"Josephine, you've been around. How many strawberries do you think would be sent to the castle?"

She turned to him wide eyed, "You don't know?"

"Well, a long time ago, when I was young, I remember eating strawberries. But… Father never ate them and Mother said they made her sad."

"Never ate them? But why would he order all the strawberries to be sent to the castle?"

"I have no idea, this is news to me. How many on average, do you think?" Josephine blinked at him her face slowly turning blank. He thought, for a moment, she wasn't going to answer him. But her eyes flickered back and forth as she seemed to imagine a strawberry field in front of her.

"It isn't going to be a good guess. I'm not firm on how many fields are in your kingdom and how often they harvest in a season. Your weather is different here from what I grew up with. One field alone, with a season I'm used to, I would say several cartful's."

"Is that all? Oh that isn't so bad."

"A *day*. At least until the season is over, which could be as long as a month or more out here."

"Oh," the prince concentrated his gaze back on the flames in the fireplace… lost in his thoughts.

The prince didn't flinch when Marie reappeared to fill their drinks, even though the cups were hardly worth refilling. Not that drinks mattered, Josephine could see she returned simply to have another glance at the man at the bar.

"Marie," Josephine began, "Who is that man you keep staring at?"

"Pardon? I have not…" The look in Josephine's eyes insisted honesty from Marie. The golden haired beauty sighed but continued, "Is it that obvious?"

"Not to him, if that helps. Who is he?"

"His name is Carlos." She swooned as she said his name. Josephine easily put her hand out to guide the poor woman smoothly into a chair. "He delivers here every day. During strawberry season he comes twice. Once in the morning with the daily food delivery, and once at night for the strawberries. He stops here for dinner before he brings to crates up to the castle."

Wendell perked up when Marie mentioned the strawberries.

"He delivers the strawberries?" the prince interrupted.

Marie looked at him a bit confused, "Well, the strawberries from this field at least."

Josephine continued as if the prince never spoke. "If he's here so often, why haven't you talked to him?"

"Well, I say hello, check off the list, and then vaguely mention something like the weather…"

The prince interrupted again, "So if he is having dinner, then the strawberries are packed up right outside, waiting to be delivered?" he stared at her to confirm.

"Um… err, yes. I suppose."

He leaned in closer. "Now, right now, there is a delivery for the castle waiting to go?"

The poor woman was frazzled, and wasn't sure how to react.

Josephine calmly put a hand on the prince's shoulder, easing him back.

"Yes, I believe that's what she said. Not to worry. He'll leave after his dinner. The poor thing has to eat."

"Besides," the waitress was regaining some confidence. "He's almost done. And he has a schedule to keep." She turned her attention back to Josephine, "Carlos is always on the go. It makes it challenging to talk about more than food or business."

"I'm sorry to hear that, Marie. I'm sure the opportunity to get to know him more will come along. You never know what the future will bring."

She smiled courteously at Josephine, but by the look in her eye she still felt forlorn at heart. "Can I get you anything else?"

The prince jumped back in the conversation once more, a bit too eagerly, "Yes!" he absorbed the glares of shock from the two women and brought his tone down several volumes. "Yes dear, please, will you send over your best dessert to the gentleman? My compliments, of course. Oh! And a quill and parchment would be wonderful, for me please."

"Absolutely!" The waitress whispered to Josephine, "Your friend is a bit odd."

She smiled back to Marie, "You get used to it. Be sure to top off whatever he's drinking too."

Marie left with a spring in her step. And Josephine turned back to the prince who was studying her with a small smirk.

"I recognize that look. Exactly, what are you planning?" Josephine asked innocently.

"I'm not sure; what are you planning?"

A smile spread across her face as her eyes lit up. After another sip of her drink, Josephine made her way towards the musicians she had recognized earlier. She easily struck up a conversation with the mend and was offered a seat at their table.

Wendell was left alone with his mouth hung open in shock. He was baffled by how easily she simply walked over and joined them. Could a smile really be all it takes to start a conversation? A kind smile perhaps, and Josephine's was perfect. Warm, innocent, sincere, with just a touch of crazy that made you want to know more about her. He shook off his thoughts and focused back on the musicians. What had once been a tired and dull lot was now teeming with conversation and laughter. One of them had even wrapped his arm around her shoulders! Wendell's gaze darkened for a moment until he saw Josephine casually lean to the side while placing the man's hand on the table instead. With an inward smile to himself, Wendell realized she would never let someone like... well, that guy... win her over so easily. Even with the obvious turn down they were still talking up a storm and having a grand time. One of the men had brought out an instrument and started showing her different fingerings; plucking a few notes so hushed only Josephine and the musician could hear. They must have been talking about something exciting because every once in a while there as a roar of laughter with Josephine clapping at what she heard.

"How does she do that?" he whispered out loud. However, the prince did not have time to dwell on the question. The waitress showed up with his drink, a quill, and some parchment. "Oh, yes, thank you Marie!" he took what was offered and started scribbling down instructions as fast as he could. He was so focused on his writing, that he hardly noticed Josephine return to her seat next to him. He had just poured some wax from a candle on to the paper and stamped his ring – leaving the royal seal in perfect view.

Josephine gave a small wave to one of the musicians who were now tuning up their instruments in the corner of the room. A few chairs have been moved to give the impression of the stage. The manager emerged from the kitchens, and was aghast upon viewing the scene in front of him. Josephine waved the man over to their table.

"What's going on?" The man asked as he eyed the musicians. He still wasn't sure if he should be excited or nervous.

"Sir, these are well known performers who have played for kings and queens all over the world! Would it be alright if they practice some of their newer songs tonight?"

"How much do they want from me?" Mumbled the owner as he scratched his beard.

"That's the best part! Since it would be a practice of only their new style of music they only ask for occasional drinks and NO requests."

"No requests! That's why people sit and listen in the first place!" he met Four's pleading expression before letting out a submissive sigh. "I suppose it would be alright… I just hope they're as good as you say they are…"

"Excellent!" Josephine gave a thumbs up to the leader and he returned the gesture with an ear to ear smile.

Prince Wendell chimed in before the owner could leave. "Since we have you here, I was asked to deliver this message to the man in charge of strawberry deliveries."

"Oh, you mean Carlos over there." The owner took one look at the message and quickly recognized the royal wax seal. "I can pass it on for you right away."

Wendell thanked him as watched the owner hurry over to the bar. Josephine watched as the note changed hands and was opened. Carlos read it, looked up to the owner, and showed him what it said. The two men exchanged confused and excited expressions as they started talking. With every word, the owner's smile grew brighter and brighter as if he might burst out of pure joy. Then, they hurried off towards the kitchens.

Josephine turned her attention back to Wendell who was gobbling up the warm stew in front of him. He broke off a piece of the bread loaf and dipped it into his bowl.

"Have you tried this bread? My goodness!"

"What was in that note?"

"Honestly, it's hearty and soft at the same time. Delicious!"

"I've tried it, yes. Now what did you do?"

"Nothing big really… I wouldn't worry about it."

"That conversation didn't look like it was about nothing."

Wendell answered her with a shrug which made Josephine slump back in her chair. She didn't say anything but eyeballed the prince with a chilling glare. This would make most people uneasy and willing to say anything to make her stop. The prince, however, had been desensitized to looks like this long ago, and easily ignored her.

"What on earth is that?" The music started up suddenly, and at an unearthly fast pace. The prince stared at the musicians in shock. How could someone's fingers possibly move so quickly? His shock turned to amazement as he realized how much work must have gone into this arrangement. Slowly… gradually, he began to like it.

"What do you think?" Josephine smiled at him.

"I've never heard anything like it!" Wendell exclaimed in a futile attempt to hide the excitement in his voice.

"No one has, this is all original. It's never been played music they have been working on."

"Why not?"

"Everyone who hires them are pretty specific with what they want to hear. There isn't much room to try out new songs. Actually, it can be pretty dull."

"Unless, some unsuspecting tavern owner is talked into letting them play their new songs… At no charge."

"You make it sound like it's a bad thing. They get to play what they want and enjoy themselves while customers spend more money while they hang around trying to decide if they like the music or not. Everyone's happy."

"I know, I see the benefits, and I enjoy hearing them too. But why couldn't they just talk to the owner themselves? Perhaps they didn't want to play tonight, you know, take a break."

Josephine's smile turned serious as she took the princes' hand gently. "Do you know why someone would choose to be a musician?"

"Because they're good at it?"

"To be heard. They're hired specifically to be listened to; to make people happy. In a way they're putting their fate in your hands. This is their chance to be heard, to put their soul out there for everyone to hear and judge and decide whether or not they would want hear them again. And when they *can* perform something they have arranged themselves, its like people are hearing them, specifically, instead of a tired composer who lived decades ago. If they're lucky, word will get around about their arrangement and maybe, just maybe, their songs will live on through history."

After a few thoughtful moments, Wendell spoke up again. "So the traditional songs are like reading to someone from a book instead of telling your own story."

"Exactly!"

"Then why didn't they ask themselves?"

She took a deep breath, "Sometimes, people get wrapped up with the way things are. They forget about the way it should be. Sadly, most reach a point where they just stop trying."

"I had no idea."

"Really? I would think this is a subject you would understand completely. Given how you handle things at the palace."

Instead of arguing with her, the prince found himself admiring her with a goofy smile on his face. There was something about how she spoke, how she held herself… Some deep intensity he had not noticed before. Whatever it was, he wanted to enjoy every second of it.

Any kind of feelings that had stirred up in the prince were stifled as the owner appeared and joined them at their table.

The owner looked intensely nervous as he talked to Wendell. "Sir, you said you worked at the palace?"

"I said I needed to deliver a message from the palace."

"Close enough. I need you to tell me when the prince arrives, please?"

"Excuse me?"

"Please, your message said that he was visiting. I want to make sure he gets the best treatment."

"You don't know what the prince looks like?" Josephine raised an eyebrow at the older man.

"Not really, they tend to stay in the palace. I imagine he looks like a younger version of his father. At least that's how I see him in my mind."

The prince sighed and rubbed his face. At least the owner's response had given him the perfect cover to stay hidden.

Wendell finally responded to the older man. "I don't know what was in that message, nor do I know what the prince looks like. Like you said, they keep to the palace. I'm just a runner, as they call me."

"Oh," the owner slumped in his seat. "What am I to do? If he's not happy I'll be out of business for sure!"

"Oh, I'm sure that won't happen," Josephine looked at the prince pleading for him to say something.

The prince was in a spot at the moment. Does he keep lying to protect himself and end up babysitting a grown man all night? Or, does he come clean and risk being surrounded by questions and business? Neither option seemed enjoyable to the prince, so he did his best to redirect the conversation.

"Dear man, get a hold of yourself." Wendell slapped the owner on the back laughing at him. "What does it matter what he looks like? He is a man. Coming to a tavern. I expect he wants something to eat and some entertainment. We aren't that complicated."

The owner glanced at the musicians who had a congregation forming around them. "I have both of those."

"Then, I suspect he will be satisfied!" Wendell shrugged as he popped some more bread in his mouth.

"Thank you," The owner nodded to his patron.

Josephine looked at Wendell in absolute surprise. "Wow, you handled that fairly smoothly."

"I do have some skills. I'm not entirely useless in this place."

"No, you are not." She agreed.

The two of them continued their discussion as they finished up their stews and allowed the music to lift their spirits even higher. Wendell missed being able to just talk with Josephine. Lately the conversation had always been about other girls and marriage prospects. He was grateful for something different to talk about. He remembered Josephine asking to do pretty much the same thing in the Fool's room. Why couldn't he have tried to understand what she was trying to say then? He shook his head at his own stupidity. Why did he allow that terrible argument, and have Josephine bring him to this tavern; to understand what should have been obvious before all of this? Then he laughed to himself when he remembered her telling him, "Sometimes the best ideas come when you're not thinking." Now, he understood its' meaning perfectly.

Chapter

13

"Do I smell strawberries?" Josephine could sense a new, sweet smell emanating from the kitchens.

The prince gave her a puzzled look, "It always smelled like strawberries in here."

"No," She saw the round little tavern owner behind the bar with a huge grin stuck on his face, then she turned back to Wendell. "I smell strawberries with sugar and spices cooking on a stove. What *was* in that message?"

The owner appeared next to Wendell again. This time he was puffed up with confidence. "I know you are just the messenger, but thank you! The prince ordered today's shipment to be delivered here," He smiled with a giddy giggle, "So he can sample some of my famous desserts!"

"Did he?" Josephine's smile grew even wider as she turned to the prince. She giggled as he blushed and sank lower in his chair. "Do you need help prepping any of your dishes?"

"Do you cook?" the owner asked Josephine.

"You can cook?" The prince asked at the same time as the owner causing them to exchange quick glances with each other.

"I know how to follow a recipe, and I am definitely good with a knife." She confidently answered.

The small little owner was overjoyed at the offer "Well come on! We'll get things moving along much faster."

Wendell looked terrified as she got up to follow the man. "You're leaving?"

"How often do you get a chance to learn how secret recipes are made? I won't stay forever, and we will have delicious pastries by the time I come back!"

"What am I going to do in the meantime?"

"Go with the flow!" She called over her shoulder with a laugh as she disappeared into the kitchen.

"Go with the flow?" He thought to himself. "Where exactly does she expect me to flow?" He grumbled to himself as he took a long drink from his mug.

"Aww… Your friend left you on your own again?" Marie asked as she filled up his drink and scooped up the empty bowls.

"She wanted to help out in the kitchens," Came his muttered reply.

"Oh my! What a sweetheart! Have you heard? The prince is visiting tonight! And Chef says there will be even more surprises to come!"

"I heard something like that."

"Then how can you still be frowning? I will admit it was dull when you first got here, but open your eyes!"

He did open his eyes, but saw nothing to lift his spirits.

"The prince is coming, strawberries that no one has been allowed to eat for years are in the kitchen, people are laughing, and music is playing! How much more do you need to crack a smile on that face?"

He stared at her thoughtfully for a few moments before blinking. He smirked. "I'll be happy when she's back."

Her eyes bored into him and read him like an open book. "Oh, now I see," She smiled knowingly. "If I were you, I would try to loosen up and have some fun; before your girl runs off with someone else." She turned and left Wendell alone with his thoughts.

The prince's eyebrows lifted at Marie's comment. She conveniently left before he could contend with her. What bothered Wendell most was no matter how hard he thought, he couldn't think of a valid argument to counter what she said. He busied himself with watching the fire to rid himself of the feeling. After sitting alone for a bit, Josephine's chair was disturbed. A large, full, man sat down next to him. It was Carlos. The prince was happy it was someone he recognized, but he was still upset yet another person wanted to come chat. Was there a sign hung somewhere inviting people over? Did Josephine tell everyone she met to come talk to him? He tried to smile, but it was awkward.

"I know you had nothing to do with the message, but I wanted to say thank you." His tone was firm and direct. Clearly, he was someone who liked to get straight to the point.

"Why is that?"

"It means I'm done for the day. I suppose it also means I can have a little fun before I head home."

"Well, you're welcome." The prince lifted his glass towards him and Carlos returned the gesture. The men drank deeply before they both stared into the fire.

"If you don't mind, can I stay here for a bit? See, it really is too early for me to turn in for the night, but I'm also a bit out of my depth with this crowd."

"I think you picked the right chair to sit in." The prince mused.

Chapter

The evening spun on filled with joy and excitement to everyone in the tavern. Eventually, Josephine emerged from the kitchen and was greeted by a different scene than the one she had left. There were almost three times the number of patrons there than before! Apparently, news about the prince visiting traveled quickly. It was either that, or the knowledge that there were going to be strawberries served since who knows how long ago. The musicians were still going strong, strumming one song after another. Many of the tables and benches had been pushed to the sides of the room to allow for dancing, and dance they did! There was a continuous crowd that filled the room, tossing and bouncing around like ocean waves. The bar had become a pastry store with a line of people waiting to point out a tasty treat in exchange for a small fee. But the most surprising development the princess saw, was finding Wendell and Carlos deeply engaged in a steady conversation near the fireplace. After gathering up a few tarts, she headed over to the men. Josephine didn't want to disturb them, but she was tired from helping in the kitchens. Besides, she wanted to enjoy the fruits of her labors. A tasty tart with the prince sounded reasonable to her. It was a small wish, but in her mind, it was a reward well earned. Thankfully, as she turned to walk back over, Carlos slapped Wendell's back, stood up, and made his way into the dancing crowd.

Josephine placed a treat in front of Wendell and sat down eagerly, impatient to taste the other in her hand.

"What's this?"

"It's a strawberry tart. It's a special one because it came from the batch I made."

"You can bake now?"

"Yup, try it!"

He took a small bite, careful to get all the elements of the dessert at once. He took his time, savoring all the flavors, textures, smell, and appearance; it was scrumptious! "Wow! This has got to be my new favorite treat." He continued on the rest of the tart greedily.

Josephine smiled, proud of her work and ready to eat. "So, what was, that, then?" She motioned with her eyes towards Carlos. He was hovering on the other side of the room meticulously watching Marie clean up dishes customers had long forgotten. He looked ready to do something, but was hanging back looking hesitant.

"Oh," The prince shrugged her off with a smile. "Just a little friendly conversation."

"Friendly conversation?" She was about to say something more when the prince quickly hushed her.

"Oh, oh! Wait, you will want to see this." He was leaning forward in his chair, hand on her arm and eyes fixed on Carlos.

Obediently, Josephine watched as Carlos's demeanor went from nervous to confident. He walked right up to Marie and took her tray out of her hands. She raced after him protesting, having to take several little steps to keep up with his long strides. Carlos gently placed the tray in a window attached to the kitchen, undoubtedly something he had seen Marie do several times now. Then, he abruptly turned around to look at her. With his now free hands, he reached out and caught her small, fragile hand in his. In a smooth motion, he kissed it gently followed by soft words. Josephine could only guess what Carlos said, but it must have been exactly what Marie was waiting for because her cheeks blossomed rosy red paired with a spectacular smile. The princess watched as the pair of them disappeared among the dancers where they would be attached at the hip for the rest of the evening.

Josephine was astounded. She never imagined the insensitive Prince Wendell to orchestrate such a tender moment. "What exactly was that 'friendly conversation' about?"

"Oh, you know, just me going with the flow, having fun."

"Huh, I never expected you to be sentimental."

"What can I say, I've got love on my mind." Wendell smiled as he relaxed in his chair.

Josephine's heart fluttered, for a moment. She looked at him longingly, wishing for her own tender scene. Instead, she found him deeply engrossed in the music. Clearly, he wasn't talking about her.

"That's right, from all those princess interviews." She responded flatly.

She looked away as the prince turned to her with the same longing Josephine just had. When he saw her focused on the music instead of him, his smile faded.

"Of course, the interviews," he muttered.

"Come dance!" One of the musicians shouted as he pointed specifically to Josephine breaking their tense silence.

Josephine smiled at the prince then eagerly ran towards the music to join the crowd.

Chapter

The prince followed every movement of Josephine like a hawk. He hated to dance, but he enjoyed watching her. Her presence alone made life more fun. In some way she transformed mundane things around her into small adventures. Everything seemed to be fun for her. This made her unlike any princess he had ever met before. Josephine wasn't like them at all. She listened to him, encouraged him, and offered help in any way she could.

Wendell sat up straighter as realization hit him. For the first time, since meeting this strange young woman, the prince was comparing her to princesses instead of just anyone. Could it be he was starting to believe her story? Could Josephine actually be the fourth daughter to a kingdom far, far away? It wasn't too hard to believe that she had traveled around from place to place serving people as she went. How else would she have known how to respond to this entire tavern situation that dealt with love, baking, bargains, and dancing? Could any kind of princess be able to handle a night like tonight the way she did? Perhaps not a princess, but a Queen could.

What was he doing? He frowned and shook the stray thought from his mind. Now he was seeing her as a queen! Perhaps the party was getting to his head, and messing with his thinking. Yes, that had to be it. He must have been caught up in the excitement and action of the moment.

Wendell's gaze drifted across the full room of people dancing, laughing, and having a good time; but his eyes always returned to her. He noticed her brow was glistening with sweat, not that it mattered. Her short hair would brush it away and leave her forehead and hair shining as light reflected off the surface. Next he noticed her smile, a smile that made it all the way from the corners of her lips to her cheeks to her eyes. She was glowing. As he continued to watch Josephine he realized he had started to smile back at her. It was the same smile she seemed to have sparked in everyone around her.

He took in all her radiance, from her smooth skin to the shape of her body. Josephine looked just like any other princess, a flawless porcelain doll, but she was different. She didn't mind getting dirty or having her careful paint smudged. Nor did she mind ending up with crack or two. Even with the cracks, she was still beautiful. When he thought more about it; the cracks, or flaws, were what made her beautiful. It showed others she regarded herself as equal to anyone else she met, flaws and all. That is why people gravitated toward her, they... loved her.

Prince Wendell was surprised by what he was now considering. Love. No, he didn't mean that... Did he? The prince looked at his cup and took a long drink, trying to calm the nerves that seemed to have come out of nowhere. It didn't work. If anything, it just made him more nervous. What was he trying to hide from

THE FOURTH PRINCESS

himself? Was it because he realized the people loved her? Or was it something else? Something deeper?

The prince rose to his feet. He needed to get out of the tavern, get away from people and the noise, and her. He broke free from the crowd and found his way outside, filling his screaming lungs with fresh air. Wendell hadn't realized he had been holding his breath until he could suddenly breathe again. Cool, moist, crisp air filled his lungs as the music died down to a soft muffle behind him.

It was blissfully peaceful out here in the quiet. All his racing thoughts had begun to slow down as had his beating heart. He hadn't realized how worked up he had gotten himself. No wonder he needed to get out. Wendell drank in the peaceful calm even deeper as he closed his eyes. One muscle at a time, he was finally able to relax. The Prince had only been out for a few seconds, but he was feeling much better.

"Are you alright?"

It was her! She had followed him outside!

Josephine's concerned voice spoke up again. "I saw you leave. I thought something was wrong."

"I'm alright. I just felt a little light headed." Her cool hand pressed against his forehead.

"You are feeling a little warm. We probably should get you home just to be safe."

"I feel fine. Your friends-"

"My friends will get along without me." Josephine finished the sentence for him. "You, Prince Wendell, are more important. Let's go."

Wendell was lost in thought while Josephine, Four, the princess, whatever she should be called, led them back. So sweet and authoritative at the same time... how could he have been so blind? He severely misjudged her. He thought back to the first day they had met. Wendell realized that comment after comment, action after action, only verified she was indeed a princess. Even when he teased her about it, she handled it better than most of the princesses he had to interact with lately. Why couldn't it be true? Was it because she would rather be out with the people and explore around than be cooped up in her parents castle studying day and night? Because she dressed for traveling instead of sitting in with the royal court for the day? Because she cares as much for those who live in the kingdom as she does for the royal family governing it? It made her unique, not unworthy of her rightful title.

Wendell noticed they were almost at the castle stables now and neither of them had spoken a word since leaving the tavern. He watched in a dazed silence as Josephine dismounted and passed her horse off to one of the grooms waiting.

"Come on," Josephine spoke. "We should get you into the castle and see if Dr. Fool can spare a few seconds."

The prince didn't move. He was so lost in thought that everything else didn't matter.

"Prince… Prince Wendell!" She shouted.

He blinked a few times and shook his head as he snapped out of his dazed state of mind and slowly came back to reality. With a sigh, he dismounted and passed his horse off as well.

The groom led the two beasts off leaving the prince and princess to their own business.

The Prince took a long sigh as he collected his thoughts.

"Well, Josephine; I suppose this means you will be leaving now that your ankle is well enough to dance on." It was hard to look her in the eye. He had finally caught up on who she was and how he felt for her… just in time to see her leave. It was all the prince could do to keep the sadness out of his voice.

Josephine stepped back looking a bit shaken by what he had said. "I suppose you're right. I should be moving on, new sights to see, people to meet."

"There are a few sights here you haven't seen yet. It would be a shame for you to miss out on them."

"Perhaps I'll linger here after I leave the castle. Do some exploring."

"Or you could stay and let me show you myself?" He suggested with a hint of hope in his voice.

"I wouldn't want to abuse your hospitality." She stopped talking as he stepped closer. Her heart fluttered.

"You are incapable of abusing my hospitality."

Wendell leaned forward just enough to wipe a few strands of her hair from her face. She blushed, as he gently took her hand in his. They stood there lost in each other's eyes for a moment.

"Your highness!" The Fool shouted, his voice paired with the steady slapping of feet on the ground. He skidded to a stop in front of the stables panting, and paused as he saw the two of them so close to each other. However, they were already stepping back away like a pair of magnets that had been flipped over. The prince found it physically painful to let go of Josephine's hand. His eyebrows raised with a perturbed expression at the Fool.

"The queen," Fool gasped out breathlessly. "She has been looking for you, she seems rather insistent."

Wendell looked at the princess longingly. He thought a moment before speaking. "It's a shame you haven't found me yet."

The Fool's jaw dropped before he could compose himself. "Of course, your highness." He bowed and slowly headed back up the path he had come with the occasional glance over his shoulder to see what would happen next.

Chapter

Back at the stables, Wendell took Josephine's hand in his. "It occurs to me that you have never really had a chance to explore the castle."

Josephine smiled, "Not really. My ankle had something to do with that, I think."

"May I give you the grand tour?"

"But, I thought you weren't feeling well."

"On the contrary, I'm feeling much better." Josephine could only smile as she allowed her hand to be wrapped around his arm.

They began their castle tour at a leisurely pace. Resolutely, calmly, they strolled through countless rooms. The prince would point out an occasional picture or structural feature that he thought was interesting. Josephine would nod and comment in turn. Eventually they went on to talk about the events of the evening.

"It felt nice to be working again."

"In the kitchens?"

Josephine smiled. "Yes, but everything else too. The owner, the musicians," She gave a broad smile, "The strawberries. It felt nice."

"You mean... what happened tonight was a normal day for you?"

"Well, they don't always pan out so beautifully. But, I try to help with what I can. Normally, I don't get the chance to see how my small little act directly affects the people around me. Nights like tonight are rare."

"I envy you," Came Wendell's soft whisper. Since they were alone in an empty room, Josephine heard him as clearly as if he spoke out loud.

"Why?"

"You do so much, help so many, all without a thought of yourself. It makes me feel like I have done nothing worthwhile."

She giggled softly at him. "Wow. And here I was jealous of you!

"You cannot be serious." He exclaimed.

"All my life I have been scrutinized, compared, weighed and measured, and I've always come up short to what was expected. It felt like no one believed in me. If I never owned up to the title of princess, how could I ever expect to become anything greater? I was never good enough so I was never given an opportunity to try to prove I could do something."

"But... that's how I feel too."

"The difference is you made your own opportunity. You run the country under your mother's nose. Everything that has happened tonight looks like a side note compared to your scroll of daily business. I'm not certain you grasp how worthwhile your life has been."

"You changed people's lives tonight."

"You change people's lives every day. Today was just the first time you saw it."

"You did most of the work there though."

Josephine shrugged. "I provided the music, you arranged the treats."

He smiled at her. "I wouldn't have known about the strawberries if you hadn't been so nosey."

"May I remind you that it was not I who sparked a romance this evening? That, my dear prince, was entirely you."

"Wrong again, you undeniably had a part in that."

"I did nothing for Marie and Carlos." She insisted in an indignant voice.

"I'm not talking about them."

"Who else fell in love tonight?"

Prince Wendell allowed a small laugh at her. "Really?"

Josephine was confused. Her mind raced a mile a minute through everything that happened that night. From the musicians to the tarts, to the dancing, then the stables. Her eyes widened for a moment before she looked away from him, her face soft and warm with a blush.

"Oh…"

Wendell kept smiling. "See? Like I said, you never think of yourself."

Josephine could feel warmth radiating from her chest as if the sun itself was trying to shine out from inside of her. "It was… quite a night," She murmured as she smiled.

The prince and his princess continued wandering through the castle speaking of many things. They smiled, they laughed, and best of all, they were happy. It was a wonderful feeling to be in the limelight of someone who genuinely cared. Sadly, as large as the castle was, the tour eventually came to an end. They had talked well into the morning hours when Wendell led Josephine out onto a large balcony filled with flowers. Hand in hand, they were greeted by a violet sky highlighted with red clouds and a splendid view of the surrounding country.

"You know, eventually I will see all of your country." Josephine smiled as she leaned against the railing.

"I'm confident you will."

"And eventually we will run out of excuses for me to stay. I'll have to move on…"

"Yes, well. I've been thinking things over and… I have an extraordinary idea."

"Really?" Josephine asked with a smile as she looked at him. She was surprised as Wendell gently pulled her off the balcony railing and scooped her hands into his. His gaze was intense and serious. There was a new glint in his eyes, something that Josephine couldn't quite place.

"I'm in love with you." He paused, drinking in her radiance. "I don't want you to leave."

The princess was taken by surprise. Of course, this was something she had day dreamed about for a while. She had fallen for the prince even before the Fool started teasing her. But, for the prince, this seemed sudden and spontaneous. Wendell was not a spontaneous man.

"Don't you have to marry a princess?"

The Prince responded gently and confident, "You are my princess."

Josephine tried to remain calm. "My parents always warned me that you can't fall in love after one pleasant evening."

"I agree with them wholeheartedly," He smiled warmly. "But, it only takes a fraction of a second to realize you *are* in love. I've been in love with you since our first day together. You inspired me to be myself and live how I want to. That's what I intend to continue doing, with you. I want you by my side as my queen. I want to keep hearing your thoughts and ideas and watch you turn things around in ways I could never imagine as possible. I'll never be happier with anyone else than I am with you."

Josephine put a hand over her pounding heart as she watched him, taking in every word and savoring it as he finished speaking. This had not been the first time someone declared their love and desires to her, but this was the first time she reciprocated that love. She heard the truth in his words so vividly. She had been wandering for so long with so many homes asking for her to stay and be a part of their lives. All were wonderful people in wonderful places she could have lived quite happily, but the timing was never right. She was never ready for a settled life. There was always so much more to see and learn, more to be done and more to give; until now. For the first time, she actually wanted to hear these words spoken to her. She felt so much love from Prince Wendell, and so much need at the same time. She had an ease around him that she had never felt before, like returning home but even better. She didn't want to see what was the next stop on the road, her adventures were right here… with him.

Wendell sucked in a nervous breath before he sank to one knee. He still had her hand in both of his. Ever so softly, her name fluttered from his mouth. "Josephine. Will you stay here with me as my wife?"

In a moment, her whole life didn't feel quite so irrelevant. She always knew herself to be a princess, daughter of a king. This, this was the first time *Josephine* believed she was more than a mere princess. She even felt she was more than a queen. For the first time she felt like… Josephine. She had blossomed into a powerful woman full of knowledge no tutor could ever teach. She had developed qualities that had been learned on her own, which made them so much more valuable. Emotions raced through her like chariots as she shook her head. Doing the best she could to calm herself, she whispered a sentence she knew would change her life forever.

"Yes, I will."

Prince Wendell stood up with a heartwarming smile then kissed her lips tenderly. The sun had risen above the horizon now and flooded the entire garden with a golden glow. They would have stayed there all day in each other's embrace to stretch that perfect moment as long as possible.

Unfortunately, that was not meant to be. All was shattered and their attention stolen away by an unbearably loud, shrill scream. Immediately their heads turned and they found Queen Katerina, Wendell's mother, staring at them practically petrified with shock.

Wendell frowned and reluctantly pulled away from the princess to calm his mother. "Hello, Mother!"

"What on earth is going on? Who is this... woman?"

"Mother, this is Princess Josephine Helena Carmina."

Josephine gave a small curtsy, similar to the one from when she first met the prince. Once again, a practically flawless curtsey appeared rather strange without the usual flowing skirts a princess would wear. The queen recoiled slightly with disgust.

"She was hurt, so she has been my guest here while her ankle healed. It was badly sprained in a storm."

"Well," The queen breathed out. "You seem to be in perfect health. It's time you were on your way. Now."

"Actually, Mother, I believe she will be staying a bit longer."

"How much longer?"

"Well," Wendell said and bounced his head from side to side in thought. "We were thinking indefinitely. See, we've become quite fond of each other. In fact," He turned to smile at Josephina, "I've fallen in love with her, and…" The queen had fainted before he could finish his sentence. He looked up at the princess and said, "Well… that went better than I thought."

Chapter

Prince Wendell had carried his mother to her private chambers while Josephine went to fetch the doctor. Within minutes the fool had arrived with his bag ready to help. The fool's countenance melted from carefree to concentration in the blink of an eye. He had shed his title of Fool and was now Doctor Kendell Krouss, hard at work. The queen awoke in a panic, heart racing and breaths short. Upon seeing she was in her own room tucked neatly into her large silken bed she was able to relax back into her pillows. All was just as it should be. The room was perfectly organized with every small object in its own special place. The drapes hung fluidly around the windows and over the bedposts, framing the room in elegance. Even the blankets on her bed hung smoothly in perfect order despite the frazzled occupant. She looked about the room and smiled deeply when she saw the doctor standing beside her. He was waving a fan to allow cool air on her face. She was grateful for it as she allowed herself a few deep breaths.

At the foot of her bed, she saw her dear son watching her. He was so handsome, not unlike how his father used to look. She saw her son was concerned. Queen Katerina smiled at Wendell to reassure him she was fine. He was so fragile. Someone needed to take care of her little boy. And though she had done her best, she would not be around forever. It was a good thing she had decided on a beautiful young princess for him to marry. Prince Wendell was so inexperienced, and lacked the command needed to take care of himself, let alone a kingdom. It was not entirely his fault. With the king's mind lost in madness, the little prince never really had a strong male figure in his life. She had done her best to mold and teach him all the things a proper king should know, but to no avail. There are some things that should only be taught by the boy's father, and that was no longer an option. The best she could do for the prince is ensure he married someone who could easily command him, and this kingdom, without flinching. Her eyes drifted on and focused in on the most unsightly thing she had ever saw.

"How dare you bring *her* into my presence!"

"Mother, she has a name. Like I said, this is Josephine. She helped us bring you here, so you would be more comfortable."

"You mean her grubby hands have touched me?!"

"Enough mother! She is a human being, not a wild animal!"

"Feral enough to be. Look at her! No manners, no confidence, no dignity. Even now she's shying away from me!"

Josephine and Wendell blinked, then looked at each other in surprise.

"My queen," Fool chimed in, "Could you please tell me the last thing you remember?"

She rubbed her temples with a heavy frown that somehow managed to make her look like a frail, damaged woman. "I recall I had a nightmare where my son proclaimed his love to some simpleton pretending to be a princess."

The fool looked up at the couple for confirmation.

"You did?" he asked unable to control his excitement.

The prince smiled at the fool while Josephine tried not to laugh.

"Mother, that wasn't a nightmare. We are in love and I fully intend on marrying her."

"Ooooooh!" The queen moaned as the fool hurried over to escort the prince and princess out. The Queen could not see the Fool's beaming grin when his back was turned away from her.

"I am so excited to hear this news! Congratulations! Honestly, Wendell, I believe this is one of the smartest decisions you have ever made. And sweet Josephine, you could not have found a more worthy man to appreciate you for all that you are. But, I think for now the queen needs some time to adjust. I'm sure she will come around; it's just a matter of time. I will see if I can calm her down."

Chapter

Josephine was comforted by the fool's excitement as the bedroom doors closed behind her and the prince. However, she could not dismiss how upset the queen was to see her. Now that she thought about it, it probably was a bit traumatizing for the queen to find her son in the arms of woman she had never seen before. Not to mention, in the arms of a woman inappropriately dressed in a tight leather outfit. For the first time in a while, Josephine wished terribly she was in a full dress with her hair pinned up in curls like her sisters.

"Do you really think she will come around?" she asked Wendell quietly.

"Of course she will. I'm not sure how, but Fool can be very persuasive with her. I'm sure he will soon have here thinking our marriage was all her idea and we won't be able to find a moment alone." She laughed at him as he took her hand. "In the meantime, we will just have to think of more things to do together without her."

******

The Queen had concealed herself in her room for several days, only allowing her closest attendants to visit. Neither Wendell nor Josephine minded her absence at all. It was nice that their secret was out. It meant no more long days hiding in the fool's quarters. It also meant no more dreadful meetings with potential brides for the prince. The two of them were free to do whatever they wished, and they took full advantage of it. They had almost forgotten about Queen Katerina sulking in her room until one day their lunch was interrupted by her personal aid. He dropped into a deep bow and announced a summons for 'the woman her son wishes to marry.'

The princesses stared at the messenger warily. "Just me?"

"Yes, my lady." The little man bowed even deeper to her as he answered.

"Is the queen in good spirits?" The prince asked.

"Yes, your highness. She is, on her feet, dressed, and laughing with her chambermaids. I can't remember the last time she was this happy."

Josephine looked up at Wendell unsure of what to make of the news. "Is 'happy' a good thing?"

"I don't see why not." Wendell shrugged. "Are you all right?"

"I'm not sure, she seemed pretty upset. I'm trying to understand how she can feel completely different about your proposal after only a few days."

"It could be a sudden change of heart. Maybe I should go with you."

Queen Katerina's aid interrupted their conversation. "I'm sorry Prince Wendell, but she only wishes to see… the lady."

They both turned to stare at the man, who shrunk a little under the weight of their glares.

Josephine spoke slowly, "I think I will be fine, I'm just not eager to see her yet."

The prince drew Josephine into his arms and kissed her gently on the lips. "I love you. Nothing she can say is going to change that. You are far too extraordinary for me to allow someone like her to keep you away from me."

Josephine smiled at him, grateful for his words. "I love you too," she whispered. "Well, I better not keep her waiting much longer."

Wendell watched her walk up the stairs towards the rooms. He couldn't help admiring her; the curve of her waist, the tilt of her neck. She was undeniably remarkable. But in times when she showed off her character, such as now, she was absolutely breathtaking. He knew she didn't want to go alone, but her courage outweighed her reservations. This was yet another trait he had come to love about her. She still had fears, worries, and insecurities just like anyone else. She would even entertain them a little, but the difference with Josephine was she controlled them. She knew in the end what had to be done, and always would set aside her fears and act as she should, steadfast in her convictions. He wondered if he had as much courage as she did, and if the time came, would he be able to stand as unwavering as her. He smiled as he reminded himself that she had agreed to be *his* wife. There must be something about him that she found worthy enough to accept. He still wasn't sure what that was, but a woman like Josephine wouldn't consent to marry anyone who she didn't view as her equal.

Chapter 40

The princess felt the butterflies in her stomach grow larger with every step. By the time she reached the queen's room she was exerting all her energy to keep from trembling. She peeked in. Sure enough, the queen was there smiling, happy, and carefree. Maybe she had come to terms with her son's decision. Despite the atmosphere in the room, Josephine still could not manage to relax even for a second.

"Come in, come in my dear." Queen Katerina sounded inviting and excited to be meeting her for a private conversation. She motioned for her to have a seat on a bench nearby. "My dear, you look so nervous," She smiled.

"A little nervous, yes. I wasn't sure what to think after our previous meeting."

"Yes, well, I hope you can forgive me. I may have overreacted. It was just a bit of anger I had to get through to be happy for you two."

"All right." Josephine wanted to relax, but every instinct she had insisted she remain cautious.

"Wonderful!" The queen stood and beckoned Josephine to follow her. "Come stroll with me in my gardens. I must have my daily exercise. You can keep me entertained by telling me all about you." She opened a glass doorway in the back of her room that was her private entrance to the garden Josephine remembered. "Now, I'm told you answer to the name of 'Four'. Why is that?"

The princess followed after the queen still massively confused by her behavior. Even more confusing is no one in this castle addressed her by the name 'Four", although she told the prince he could do so. "It is a nickname I've been given. I've used it for a while, and I have grown to like it."

"Surely Queen Laurel never called you that."

"I'm not sure she even knows I answer to 'Four'." Josephine gave the queen an odd look. How did she know who her mother was? She had mentioned her father's name to Wendell, but none of that had been told to the queen.

Queen Katerina could see the princess had grown uneasy, and allowed herself a sly smile of triumph. "You are much more known that you realize, dear girl. It would seem there's a story about a 'Fourth Princess' just about everywhere now. People talk about her as if she were a hero who arrives to make all their worries disappear. You are something of a legend."

"I wouldn't really call my stories *legend*," Josephine blushed.

"Nor would I, but I started to pay closer attention when I heard your parents have been looking for you."

"My parents have been looking for me?"

"Of course they are. How long were you planning on avoiding them?"

"I'm not avoiding them. I had no idea they were looking…"

"If you're not avoiding your family then why are you wandering around the world looking for reasons to be away from them?" The queen's voice, though still pleasant, had taken on a sharp tone.

Josephine paused for a moment while the queen continued to stroll deeper into the gardens. She wanted Queen Katerina to stop and speak to her face to face. The conversation had moved beyond a mere idle chat on a leisurely stroll. Stopping was not an option for Josephine though. The further Josephine allowed the queen to walk ahead the closer her rear guards came up behind her. It was then that she realized that there was a guard at every twist and turn that they walked by. Each one keeping a tight eye on Josephine. She hurried to catch up with the queen, trying to add more distance between her and the rear guard. Unfortunately, the men kept up with her steps easily, and continued to stay close to her heels.

"I didn't want to sit around my parents' castle waiting for them to marry me off. I wanted to do something more with my life, so I decided to leave."

"So you admit to leaving your family and all royal obligations?"

"My only royal obligation was to get married, and I wasn't ready for that. I wanted to know what I alone was capable of before I settled down with someone for the rest of my life. And my family was perfectly fine with my decision." Josephine looked around and noticed the guards were even closer to her now. "If you don't mind, I would like to return to Wendell now. He's probably wondering where I am." She tried to curtsey and take one of the turns that led back to the castle, but as soon as she tried the guards surrounded her, with hands grasping the hilts of their swords.

The queen finally stopped her stroll long enough to turn and look at Josephine. There was a menacing fire in her eyes.

"I think it would be best if you stayed close to me, Princess Josephine." Queen Katerina spat her name as if the words tasted bitter in her mouth. "My son needs to marry someone who will bring out the best in him. Someone who can lead him properly towards correct decisions. I do not believe that person is you."

"And you believe you know me well enough to come to this conclusion?"

"Oh, I already know all about you princess. The tragic tale of King Ronald the Second and Queen Laurel's youngest daughter running away. The pressures of ruling a kingdom – just too much for her. Shunned by her sisters and a disappointment to her parents. I wouldn't stay either." The queen had led her around a turn away from the gardens. Josephine could see they had entered into a maze of high stone walls curving every which way. She also noticed the walls getting taller and taller as the slope of the paths wound down into the earth. The queen's pace remained steady and consistent.

The walls seemed to close in on Josephine as she followed the queen. She wanted to run. She *needed* to run as far from the queen as possible, but there was no opportunity. She had walked right into the middle of whatever trap Queen Katerina planned for her. Josephine remained composed, unwilling to allow the queen to see her defeated in any way.

"That is a tragic story." Josephine responded curtly. "I'm happy it isn't mine."

"You deny you are Josephine, fourth daughter of King Ronald the Second, princess of Ebren?"

"I do not deny who I am, but that story is riddled with lies and exaggerations. I am not shunned by my sisters and neither did I run away from my parents."

"You didn't disappoint them in your studies, proving yourself inferior to your sisters?"

"I was…" the princess was surprised by what the queen knew. "I was quite successful in my studies. I believe we all have something to offer. Each one of us have different strengths as well as our own weaknesses."

"How you have romanticized your family relationship. Do you really believe your sisters, who are married and have moved on to more important things, still care about you? To them, you are just their little sister who has run far, far, away from her home and her duties."

"It is because I am their sister that I know they *do* care. I'm unclear who your sources are, or how they acquired this information, but you are severely misinformed."

The queen continued to lead her through an archway that cut deeper into the ground. It turned into a natural cave that had been modified with carved out rooms fashioned with iron bar doors. Josephine knew exactly where they were headed. She had allowed herself to be led straight to the dungeons. Her blood began to boil as the queen continued down several cascades of stairs that had been carved out.

Josephine continued, not wanting to be led to her capture in silence. "Now, before you continue with your lies, and attempt to ruin the image I have of my parents, I would like to say they would be proud of me. I've done a lot of work for many people over many kingdoms. It may not be the ideal task for a princess, but even my parents will agree it is better than sitting in a castle all day long waiting for something to happen."

"Yes, approval from dear Mom and Dad. Something you have not had the pleasure of."

"With all due respect, my queen," Josephine spoke up defensively. "You do not know myself or any of my family well enough to make accusations such as these."

The queen rounded on her with an assertive tongue. "I know my son is in love with a woman who is so uncomfortable with herself she won't even use her own name. A woman who is ashamed of her name is ashamed of her past and that includes your family. Stuck in the shadows of your predecessors, you want someone to see you as extraordinary and the more you try to make your mark in this world the further you come up short. Regardless of how much my son loves you, I would rather die than hand my kingdom over to your uncertain and incapable hands!"

Josephine glared at the queen wanting desperately to say something clever that would cut straight at Katerina's heart. Instead, Josephine could only answer with silence. When the queen finally stopped, Josephine found herself standing on the edge of a cliff deep underground in a large cavernous room. On the other side of the cave attached to the wall was an outcrop of stone that made a small platform.

The queen waved her hand and a delicate rope bridge lowered to span the gap from the cliff to the platform on the other side.

Josephine's palms began to sweat. Her voice waivered as she asked, "Where have you taken me?"

"This is my oubliette." Queen Katerina announced proudly, as her voice echoed off the walls. It is a place for forgetting." The queen motioned Josephine to cross the bridge as her guards closed in to dissuade any disobedience from their prisoner.

Josephine swallowed nervously, but turned and crossed silently. The bridge was so unstable that the sturdy platform at the end was welcoming. The princess hadn't realized she had been holding her breath until she had both feet safely on the sturdy structure across the void. Josephine relaxed for a moment, but as she turned around to face the queen the blood in her face drained in pure terror. The unstable bridge was being taken away once more leaving her trapped on the platform by the cool air swirling up from the dark abyss.

"And just what am I supposed to forget while I'm here?"

"Nothing. My son, however, will eventually forget about you. When he does, you are free to go."

"You are mad, woman!" Josephine protested in frustration, tears were stinging at her eyes, threatening to spill out. "Like it or not, we love each other. He will find me! He will never forget about me!"

The queen's manner grew as cold as the cave. "Then you will never leave."

"Stop! Let me out of here!" Josephine's cry was answered by the sound of an iron door slamming, noisily into place and then, nothing. Her shouts became mere echoes in the void that crushed down on her. Each sound she made mocked her in return and settled heavily on her shoulders. This was a situation she had never been in before, and it terrified the princess. She was alone for the first time in her life, truly alone.

Chapter

Back in the palace, Prince Wendell had been pacing the hallways ever since he let Josephine slip out of his sight. "What could they be saying?" He wondered. The thought chewed at his mind worrying him, angering him, depressing him. There were a number of things they could be discussing and each possibility brought one disturbing feeling after another.

Out of the corner of his eye, he saw his mother strolling out of the gardens. Anxiously, he turned to watch for the princess to follow her; she wasn't there. She wasn't there at all. "Mother!" He ran to meet up with her before she disappeared into another room. The prince knew something was wrong. "Where's Josephine?"

"I'm sorry, my boy," the queen whispered. "She has left."

"Left?" The prince could not believe it. He scowled at his mother. "What did you do?"

For a moment, Queen Katerina was surprised by the venom in his voice, but she answered him innocently.

"Me? I didn't do anything."

"You must have said something then." Prince Wendell looked at her demanding answers.

"I only told her how I've realized she would be a great addition to our kingdom and I apologized for how I acted towards her. Then we started talking about a royal wedding." The queen took a rehearsed breath to emphasize what she would say next. "I think she realized a marriage would tie her down in one place. Josephine told me she must move on in order to pursue her love of service to those around her."

"That's ridiculous! What better way to serve the people and the neighboring countries than to be in a position of power to help them?"

"Oh my son, it is a shame she decided to choose everyone else, over you. Josephine doesn't appreciate you as well as you deserve. I am sure one day you will learn to forgive her for it."

Wendell heard everything his mother said clearly, but couldn't believe it. "But... she loves me." The prince whispered to himself as the wheels turned frantically in his mind, piecing together the information and trying to form a solution. He looked up with a sudden, jerked movement. "I must go after her!"

Queen Katerina's mouth gaped and eyes bulged. "What?!" She snapped a little too sharply which caused her to break her false sympathy.

"I need to find her, remind her of all the good she can do here. I must prove to her that I do love her and I need her by my side, forever. I cannot let her leave."

"But sweetheart," the queen began running after her son to keep up with him. "She has made her choice. She's chosen her simple life instead of you. You cannot tell her to leave that. How do you know she even loves you?"

"She does love me, and I love her. That is the one thing I am positively convinced of."

"If she loved you then she wouldn't have left. She's a fickle woman. If you find her, she will only break your heart!"

"Staying here pent up in my comfortable castle while I simply allow her to leave, will break my heart!" The prince found his way to the stables and started outfitting his horse.

"My boy! You cannot leave like this!" She protested and tried to stop him.

"And why not?"

"You have no food or water, no provisions of any kind! You don't even have a change of clothing!"

Wendell ignored her and mounted his horse. "Did she say where she was headed?"

"No but... Wendell! This is madness! I don't want to lose you to bandits or wolves or-"

She was cut off by the Prince who was ignoring her protests entirely. "She came in from the east so I will continue west, up the coast. Yes. I believe she would have gone there next."

"You will die within the week for sure!"

"Then again," he continued thoughtfully. "If she's upset, she could want to be around more familiar territory and people. No, to the west... She would want a fresh start with no pressure." He turned to his mother with new resolve. "Don't worry mother. If she can travel light, then so can I. I will find her and bring her back home." He turned and kicked his horse into a run before the queen could utter another word.

The queen stood there in absolute shock as she watched her son ride off in search of a princess who was hidden deep in the dungeons. The Queen was paralyzed with fear.

"What... have I done...?"

Chapter

The fool was deep underground, beneath the royal gardens. He needed somewhere dark where he could see the color and patterns of his little experiments. After much searching, he found the dungeons. He started in there, but felt awkward working on explosions in such a confined space. In addition, he was nervous he would accidentally lock himself in one of the cells, and be forgotten about. Interestingly, he had discovered smaller but distinct paths that led further into the cliff. A few led to large open caves that gave him plenty of room to practice and test new ideas. It was a lucky find, and he was proud of himself because of it. Not only that, but the caves were hidden away nicely, so he could retreat from the buzz of the castle whenever he wanted. He had finished a few explosions with great success when he heard a tiny voice echoing through the cave walls followed by a few sharp clicks. Curiously, the old man followed the voice further into the tunnels.

"Hello!!! I can hear you, please!!! Help me!!!" Followed by more clicks.

The fool followed the noise to an unguarded door. It sounded like the voice was coming from there, or at least he hoped it was coming from there. The door was locked, of course, so he peered in through a barred hole in the top half of the door. That's when he saw her, the Princess Josephine, smacking rocks against the wall and crying out into the darkness that surrounded her.

"Help me! Please!" Her hoarse voice scratched against the stone around her. "Whoever you are!"

The fool was stunned. "Josephine!" He shouted through the window.

She paused and squinted at the door. "Doctor? Is that you?" Hope welled up inside of her. "Get me out!"

"I can't. It's locked – some kind of puzzle code. Who did this to you?"

"The queen! She tricked me with apologies about her behavior earlier and we ended up here. She's keeping me hidden until the prince forgets about me…"

"All because she thinks you aren't a princess?" The fool asked with an odd look.

"No, it's strange. She knew everything about me already. She knew my family, my parents! I don't know how!"

"She knows who you are?" The fool's eyes grew wide in terror. "Don't worry Josephine. I'm going to find the prince and get you out of there."

"Oh! Thank you Doctor Fool!"

He hurried back up to the dungeons, further up and up until he reached the ground level. Then a straight sprint to the castle. His body started to ache but he didn't slow down. All that mattered was finding the prince and getting Josephine as far away from the queen as possible. If she knew Josephine's true identity then this anger was more than a mother's disapproval, this was vengeance. He started to mutter to himself, "This is bad, this is so, so bad."

He was so focused on finding the prince that he nearly ran into the queen coming in from the stables. He caught himself so he wouldn't crash into her. The clumsy movement sent him tripping over his own feet and tumbling to the ground.

"Fool." The queen stared at him and glanced at the direction he came from. "What are you up to?"

Fool pushed himself up and carefully regained his balance before bowing. It allowed him some time to settle on a story. "Your Highness," He bowed again awkwardly. "I have been working on a special presentation, for the prince, for some time now. I had hoped to display it at his wedding to the Princess Josephine. The prince wanted me to inform him when I had my first successful test. Do you know where I can find him?" He bowed again trying to look as clumsy as ever, so she wouldn't read too much into his story.

"Where are these tests taking place?" Her eyes narrowed.

"In the dungeons of course," He confessed. "I'm dealing with fire and the dungeons are damp and won't allow anything else to catch and turn into a scene. Plus, tell me any other place that's dark enough during the day, so I can see patterns and lights in the explosions I create, hmmm?"

She continued to stare then gave up as she rolled her eyes. "The prince has left the castle. I am not certain how long he'll be gone."

"What!?" The fool blurted out.

She gave him an icy stare at his lack of respect.

"You're Highness." He gave another comically deep bow. "Forgive me, but will there be no wedding for my display?"

The queen considered the fool for a while and cracked a smile at him. The grin sent a cold chill down his spine. Her answer to him was loud enough for all her nearby attendants to hear. "Keep working on your display. I want it perfect. The prince has informed me that when he returns he shall marry Princess Olivia straight away. We must be extra vigilant on preparations for we do not know when he will return." She gave the fool one last look before she moved on, followed by her entourage.

The fool remained in his low bow, paralyzed by his thoughts. "The prince chooses *now* to leave on some quest?!"

Chapter

Josephine had been waiting almost an eternity before the fool returned again, or that's how it felt to the isolated young woman. Time crawls by when there is not much to do, aside from entertaining her own thoughts. Occasionally, the princess would peer over the edge of the cliff, but the scenery never changed. The dark void would snatch at her chest making it a struggle to breathe. She was not used to being so confined. True, she had all the air and space she could ever need. But, for a woman who is used to being up and about, constantly working on something, ready to get on the move again, the empty space crushed in on her from all sides. To her, the weight was heavier than any shackle that could bind her. She was able to breathe easier when she heard the fool return to the door, but her hopes of a quick rescue were all in vain. Her spirits fell in a shattered heap as he explained everything he learned.

"He... left?

"I know! The boy has never set one toe off the castle grounds. All of a sudden he chooses now to hop on a horse and disappear at the drop of a hat."

Josephine's legs crumpled beneath her. With Wendell gone, her dreams of a speedy rescue, and possibly her new life as his wife began to wither away. Only the fool remained, and he was on the other side of a locked door across a deep and dark chasm that would cause her to panic should she look over the edge.

"What do I do now?" She asked softly, her voice carrying well in the empty space. Her eyes stung as she allowed them to well up a bit.

"You are going to stay strong and not let the queen break you. The prince has to return sometime. We will figure this out." The fool was quiet for a moment, but Josephine knew by the rustling sound he was working on something. "Now, stand back for a second," he shouted so she could hear. The princess scarcely had a second to duck underneath a ball of dirt that whizzed over her head and violently splattered against the wall.

"What on earth!?"

She was answered by another ball of dirt smashing over her head. Dirt rained on top of the poor princess and spilled over the edge of the raised area she stood on. Finally, a small ball of dirt landed smoothly in front of her and rolled forward, nudging her foot. She picked up the ball. It had started as mud that had been left to harden into shape.

Josephine furrowed her brow, confused. "How is a mud ball going to help me?"

"Oh, that was just me sighting the launcher. Here comes a gift. Try to get them before they fall."

Josephine heard a distinct *kathunk* and saw a small pouch soaring towards her. She easily held out her hands to catch it.

Before she had a chance to figure out what is was, she heard the fool shout, "Another one!"

The same *kathunk* sounded softly and a second pouch soared smoothly into her outreached hands. Each pouch felt about the same weight as the ball he had launched earlier.

"What are you doing with a launcher?" She asked.

"It's a smaller version of the launcher we were working on together. Remember, it was hard to see some of the explosions when we just lit them on the ground. Now they can have plenty of space in the sky. I have to say, most of them look far better when viewed that way."

She smiled. "You mean it works? Very nice! I hope to see them someday." She opened each pouch and looked inside. The first had a round flask filled with water; the other, however, was a bit less exciting, "Peas?"

"It was the only thing I thought no one in the kitchens would miss."

She allowed herself a smile for the fool. She would not have minded if her parents' supply of peas had disappeared from the kitchens while growing up either. But the gesture was more than generous, and she was starting to get hungry.

"Thank you."

"I need to get back now. I think the queen is already suspicious of me once she realized I was working down here. I specifically came here so that I could do my work alone without anyone's eyes watching me. I suppose she had the same idea for you. I'll be back tomorrow though, I'll come every day if I can manage it. And don't worry, I'll keep a sharp eye out for Prince Wendell when he returns. Whatever happens, don't lose hope."

"I will do my best, thank you."

Josephine tried to get comfortable as she leaned against the wall. She started to eat with a slow nibble on her peas and sips from her water determined to make both last. There must be some way out of here, but she couldn't see it, not right now. The princess closed her eyes and wished with all her heart. "My prince, wherever you are, please come find me."

*****

On the other side of the prison door, the Fool was gathering up his things. He frowned as Princess Josephine's soft words rang loud and clear in his ears. Seeing the Princess Josephine locked up had upset him beyond reason. The queen had done this and he was certain to some degree it was his fault. He was going to do whatever he had to, to help the princess. He felt obligated to do so, not for Josephine, but for her mother.

Chapter

The prince rode long and hard. By twilight, the border of his kingdom was far behind him, and he was ready to stop for the night. Wendell was grateful for the directions to a cozy, little inn a passerby gave him. He couldn't wait to fill his belly and put his feet up. Upon entering the inn, he immediately sat down at the bar to satisfy his thirst before he turned and looked around the room. All the patrons seemed to be larger, hard working men. Wendell stuck out like a sore thumb with his relatively clean clothing and smaller frame. His hands even looked dainty compared to the calloused hands of the men around him. To make matters more interesting, they all had their eyes fixed on him. The bartender was the first to speak.

"You're a long way from home, stranger." His deep, gravelly voice made Wendell feel uneasy. It took everything he could muster not to tremble. He forced calm thoughts into his mind

THE FOURTH PRINCESS

to ease his nerves. The last thing he wanted here in front of all these men was for them to perceive him as weak.

"You have no idea."

"So what would drag a fine, young man out to this side of the forest?" the bartender asked. The prince did not miss the tone of loathing in his description.

He remembered Josephine's example to always keep to the truth. He wasn't sure how it would help him in this situation as the men seemed to be crouching closer and closer, ready to pounce.

"Why not." The prince leaned forward and locked eyes with the bartender. "I'm looking for someone very special to me. Her name is Josephine, but she also goes by the name of Four. I think she's also known as 'The Fourth Princess.'"

The bartender leaned in closer, so his bulbous nose was almost touching the prince's. You could hear a pin drop in the room as he asked, "What do you want with her?"

Wendell felt his fingers start to tremble as he swallowed. "I… want to marry her."

A wave of laughter crashed into the room. Each man had relaxed significantly and the room roared with their voices again.

One of the men at the bar slapped the prince's back with a hearty, "You and everyone else here!"

The bartender lobbed a loaf of bread down on the counter next to the prince with a chortle. "Let's give the lad some food for his… noble quest."

"What's so funny?" The prince demanded, hushing the crowd a bit.

"Not a day goes by that some naive young man, such as yourself, shows up heart in hand to give to the Fourth Princess." He snorted, "As if they're expecting her to be waiting for them *here*! They hear the rumors about her, and all they can think is to marry her. It's amusing to see how many fools think they are worthy enough to win her heart."

The prince wilted a bit. Was he worthy enough for her? "What are these rumors? Will you tell me?"

"What rumors? You never heard of how she stared down an entire army into surrender? Or the time she made it rain, bringing life back to crops that had long since started withering away." He threw up his arms in exaggeration, "She danced for the Lord of Tymes to slow down the sun in order for their Winter Moon Jubilee to last longer!"

"Wow!" The prince was astonished. "When you put it like that, she sounds… magical."

The bartender immediately turned serious as he locked eyes with the prince.

"Indeed she is," the bartender emphasized. From the expression on his face and the way he held himself, the prince had a feeling this man knew more than what he was saying.

"I'm not sure if she did all of that, but I do know the woman I'm looking for did prevent a war. She also helped several farmers learn how to irrigate their crops by diverting a stream. And I believe she mentioned a party that lasted several days, but I'm positive she didn't stop the sun."

The bartender spoke slowly, still stone serious as before. "How do *you* know this?"

"Because she told me."

"You mean you actually know Four? You have met her, talked with her?"

Wendell looked up. "Yes. I do, I have; and judging by your words, you know her too." By now, the room had settled into its normal atmosphere as people talked and laughed, enjoying each other's company.

THE FOURTH PRINCESS

The bartender leaned to the side, considering the prince for the moment. Without a word he turned and unpinned a letter from the wall behind him. "I haven't had the pleasure. My brother knows her, he's a few kingdoms over. She was staying with them when his wife went into labor." He allowed a long pause before continuing. "You have to know, they had been pregnant many times before, always with complications and a tragic loss. This time wasn't any different. But… the princess was actually able to carefully cut the child out, safely mind you. Then, she sewed Anabelle back up. My sister-in-law looks like she had been sliced in half, but she doesn't care. None of that matters in the end. They have a beautiful, healthy baby girl. I have a niece! Their most desperate and loving wish came true, and it's all thanks to her." He looked up with defiance in his eyes, "Do you dare dismiss that as anything but magical?"

The prince realized he was staring at the man, mouth open, in awe at his story. He blinked once or twice as he focused on the bread in front of him. "I knew she helped deliver a baby. The rest… you're right, it is magical. I'm so glad they're doing well."

The bartender watched him closely for a few seconds. "Why do you want her? There are many other women, even other princesses to choose from. Is she just another dragon you need to slay, to prove your worth?"

The prince frowned as he thought for a moment. "Was she?" He was so busy thinking about what he wanted, he forgot about her. She seemed happy enough when she was with him. She had said "yes" to his proposal instead of running away. But she did run away, later, after she had time to think. Then something his mother told him invaded his thoughts in her eerie voice. "… she must move on in order to pursue her love of service to those around her."

"I love her," He answered softly. "I know she loves me too because she told me, but she just left without notice. She's not the kind of woman you allow to just slip out of your life without reason. After all she's done, I wouldn't think of myself as a man, if didn't at least try to go after her. At least then, if she denies me, I will know firsthand it is what she wants, and she will be happy."

"Well, I like your answer, but we haven't seen her. I will set you up with a meal and a room as long as you're on your way before dawn."

"That would be wonderful. Thank you, sir."

Chapter

Josephine sat as dignified as ever on her stone throne. An onlooker would never have realized she was being held there as a prisoner with a slim chance of being rescued. She had tried to keep track of the days; but, with no point of reference, it was hard to judge how long she had been trapped. What she wouldn't give to see the sun again, or the moon, or even a star. Doctor Fool had promised to visit every day, but it proved harder in actuality. The queen had assigned a guard to assist the fool in his work. She told him the guard was to ensure his display was an absolute success for the prince's wedding to Princess Olivia. What she actually meant was she wanted someone to keep an eye on him for her. He had managed to come see Josephine a second time with more peas, water and information, but after that, he had to hurry back. The princess was very grateful for every minute he was able to sneak away. Hearing her friend's voice gave her the extra strength she needed to hang on a little longer.

At first, she decided to use this time in forced isolation to meditate, and that had worked well for a little bit. However, the cold rock was hard on her body, and sitting in meditation was getting too painful. She let out a soft chuckle into the piercing silence as a thought crossed her mind. "If only there was a way to get a mattress in here. I wouldn't feel as cold and my backside wouldn't hurt so much." The echo of her laugh died away leaving her alone in silence with her thoughts once more. It didn't last long. The princess found her concentration shattered as the sound of metal scraping back and forth made her jump out of her skin. Quickly, she stashed the four pouches into her pockets and stood as if she were receiving an honored guest. She was a little surprised to be graced with a visit from the queen along with her usual procession of royal aides and guards. It was an odd thing for the queen to do, especially when Josephine was put down here specifically to be forgotten.

"How are we feeling today, my dear?" It was horrifying how light her voice sounded. The princess was disgusted by how pleasing this was for the queen.

"Your highness, I did not expect a visit from you so soon. I gather you're here because the prince has forgotten me already?"

The queens' lip curled into a sneer at such a thought. "Still as defiant as ever I see."

Josephine held out her hands. "Simply stating the facts."

"The one trait which you are good for." The queen smiled in triumph when the princess did not answer in turn.

Josephine wanted to scream at her. So much anger frothed up inside with every word from that woman. But, that would achieve nothing. If she did plan on escaping, eventually, she would need to keep a level head. She would also need to think of something, anything, except the pain of the rock hard floor. Josephine found joy in comparing Wendell's mother to the stone walls that surrounded her, unyielding and just as painful. Now that she thought about it, just about every mother has that impression given the right circumstance. She thought of her own mother. Immediately, the princess remembered a hard lesson her mother taught her long ago.

"I find it ironic, your highness, that a queen so preoccupied on how a princess should act cannot demonstrate those qualities herself."

Queen Katerina balled her fists, "You insolent…"

"Sure the overall presentation and mannerisms are correct, but the general study is a bit lacking."

"How dare you imply such a thing!"

Even with the dim lighting surrounding her, Josephine could see Queen Katerina's face turn a deep shade of red. "Merely sticking to what I'm good at: the facts. Another fact, someone who has studied would know all about The Royal Guide to War. In this case, prisoner treatment. Honestly, my parents had me learn this when I was twelve."

"There is no such book," The queen said evenly. She knew she was being trapped but wasn't sure how to proceed.

The princess spread her hands, to appear as meek as possible. "As you say, your highness. You would certainly know more than a young little know-it-all." Josephine stood with all the confidence and elegance she could muster waiting for the queen to leave, instead, she took the bait.

"And, pray tell, what do you claim this book says about prisoners?"

Josephine worked hard not to smile. She spoke again as if reciting the text as written. "The Royal Guide to War states: 'Every prisoner must be allowed a bed. Otherwise they may die due to exposure or disease. Should this happen, the use of the prisoner is obsolete and your advantage deterred due to the waste of resources in the effort to initially capture, and store said prisoner. Therefore, it would have been better if the prisoner had been killed directly and made an example of rather than endure the unnecessary pain and torture of their superior's incompetence.'"

The other side of the chasm was very silent. Josephine waited and felt her confidence slowly escape her with every silent second. The queen stood there considering her.

Unexpectedly Queen Katerina started to laugh as she waved one of her aides over to her. Upon hearing her instructions he straightway disappeared into the hallway.

"You're asking me for a bed?" The queen continued to laugh. "Of all the things to ask for!" Josephine stood her ground and did not allow the queen to disarm her.

Amused, Queen Katerina turned to the rest of her aides and whispered more instructions. Then, after collecting her poise she faced the princess. "Dear, foolish, girl, if a bed is all you desire than you shall have it! And to prove to you how gracious I can be, I shall give you twelve. I want to ensure that you are as comfortable as possible in your misery."

Gears were turned and the all too familiar ramp was lowered again to form a bridge across the chasm. Each returning aide had more trouble crossing the bridge than the princess did, thanks to the mattresses they carried. The queen continued to laugh at the princess's stupidity. Her cackles bounced off the cave's walls, and each echo layered on top of the other. The sound disturbed Josephine as the expansive room made her feel as if an entire crowd were laughing at her expense. For a second she did feel foolish, causing her to worry as the aides continued with their work. One bed was fine, but twelve? She would have to climb to reach the top, assuming she didn't fall into the abyss on her way up. On top of that, the room on the ledge had been reduced drastically allowing her barely enough room to sit with her legs outstretched if she wished.

Once the servants were finished and the ramp taken away, the queen nodded indignantly at the princess. "As you requested, little princess." She turned and left the room, her procession in tow.

Josephine was stunned by just happened. The queen hand managed to turn her request into a burden as her situation was not much better. On the other hand, she had been able to trick the queen into granting that request. Now, that was something she was proud of and had to remember in case the queen ever returned. She placed her fists on her hips as she stared up at the heavy tower of fluff. "Well, I have my bed. Now what?"

Chapter 25

The prince strolled down a winding road along the foothills of a mountain. He was weary from riding all day with still no town in sight. There were no homes, farms, or buildings of any sort that he could find rest in. Ordinarily, this would be a dreadful situation for the prince. A perfect reason to stay in his own kingdom, within the walls of his own castle, where he wouldn't need to worry about where he would be sleeping that night. But, since he met Josephine, his eyes began to see things a little differently. He thought of what the princess would be thinking if she were there with him. He thought of her smile. Josephine would feel weary for sure, but she would still be smiling. She would discover some way to transform the day into an adventure, or anything better than this. Her smile came back to him, her lips, and then her eyes. Her eyes were bright and full of wonder, but when she smiled it awakened so much more.

Her entire frame would become a blaze of excitement, love and warmth. The image of her was so definite that he could actually feel warmth flow from his memory of her. He scanned the low meadow below him, and he saw the crimson sun on the horizon adorned with purple and pink wisps of color. Now *he* was smiling. The view was breathtaking for sure, but the smile was for her.

As the sun lowered on the horizon his spirits fell with it and the reality of his situation struck him again. It was going to be harder to trek across such a rocky terrain with his light slowly dimming on him. It was almost dark, he knew he needed to stop, but where? The darkness answered his question. The darker it grew small fires appeared, one by one, in the distance. He steered his horse off the road and onto the soft grass. The lights seemed welcoming and warm. Upbeat, energetic music grew stronger as he drew near.

It was a traveling group of performers. Every little fire was encircled by wagons of families and friends preparing to have their dinner. Laughter filled the air now that they were able to sit back and relax after a hard day of traveling. A little boy shouted to the group as soon as he saw the prince and ran over to his parents. There was an awkward pause from the camp of performers before an organized sort of frenzy broke out. Men and women with drawn bows, knives, and even hammers surrounded Wendell as he was escorted into the middle of the camp.

An old and wrinkling woman with long silvery hair sat in front of her wagon. Her dress seemed to be a puzzle of materials all patched together oddly with elegant, ornate stitching. The colors blurred together in a rainbow as she walked toward him. The old woman stood, hands on her hips, waiting for him to do something.

The prince bowed as formally as he could. "My lady, I am a simple traveler on my way to the next city. I was drawn to you by your fire in the hopes that my horse and I may rest with you for the night."

"Lies," One man hissed. "Traveler, yes, but simple he is not."

"Who are you really," A wiry man asked.

The prince took a deep breath as he heard Josephine's voice in his head again. *Stick to the truth.* "I am Prince Wendell of Tridith."

"A little far from home aren't you, little prince?" a woman mocked and the crowd started to laugh.

The old woman held up her hand as she studied Wendell for a long moment. Everyone hushed, and waited.

"Whoever you are, I can see you mean us no harm. And if you did, you are too weak to do anything about it." This made a few men laugh to themselves as they lowered their weapons. "You will share my fire, and you will tell me your story."

In an instant, everyone was back to what they were doing before he showed up; although, many stayed close to learn more about him. Even then, they were all laughing and entertaining each other as others brought over some soups that had been boiling. They watched their guest closely as the old woman offered him a seat next to her. "Are you hungry?"

The prince smacked his lips. "A little, but you needn't worry about me. I have…"

"We will share our meal if you sing." she stated loudly for all to hear.

"Sing? No that's not necessary. I don't sing well at all."

"Then you will play."

A guitar was held in front of him. Everyone looked insistent that he do something. He couldn't say no again.

"I am pretty good with the guitar." He smiled as warmly as he could. The prince's smile faded into nervousness when the members of the camp drew in closer to hear what he would play. Wendell quietly plucked a few strings, and then played the first song he could think of. It was the one he was playing when Josephine showed up, and changed his life in so many ways. He missed her terribly. The prince had been on the road for weeks, and still no sign of her. Her rumors, now practically a legend, followed him everywhere. At first, he loved each story. He would go out of his way to seek out any new detail to learn more about Josephine's life before him. Now they were getting harder to hear. With each incredible insight into her life before the prince, doubt started to ensnare him. Why him? Nothing he has ever done in his life could shine a candle in comparison to the legacy she has left. Why would she want to give this all up for him? Could he *allow* her to give this life up for him? He finished his song and handed the instrument back. A few people clapped, most just stared in uncomfortable silence. The prince cast his eyes down in shame.

The old woman cleared her throat. "You play beautifully, but your song is melancholy. Why?"

The prince sighed. "I have been searching for a friend of mine, and am having no luck."

"This friend, who is he?"

"She. Her name is Josephine, but she likes to be called Four, or the Fourth Princess."

The group was abuzz with everyone talking quietly to each other. The prince wasn't surprised they recognized the name, but he already knew they haven't seen her. No one he met had seen her, but everyone knew her stories.

"You know Four's given name?" The old woman leaned closer to him. "Are you her family?"

"No, I am…. a friend."

The old woman's eyes narrowed. "It is a long way to travel for a friend."

"Well… I'm a good friend?"

"You mean her lover." The old woman glared.

"Why do you say that?"

"Because of your song." The answer came out so obviously that the prince felt like he had been sucker-punched in the gut. He rubbed his face in his hands.

"Why must you be so dreary? Love is a thing to celebrate!" The old lady was trying to cheer him up.

"I did celebrate it. We were very happy, until she was unnerved by something that was said and she left without saying good-bye."

Her brow furrowed. "That does not sound like our princess at all. She would never leave without a reason."

"Oh, I'm sure she had a reason." The prince mumbled.

The woman smirked, "Yes, but she would have told you. She absolutely loves to talk." This made the prince laugh as he relaxed a bit.

"How do you know The Fourth Princess?"

"She danced with us for a season. Lovely dancer, but her true talent is poetry. She had a way with words that could tug at any feeling she wanted. All her work was turned into songs. Some of our best are from her! Oh yes, everyone adored her, no matter where we went."

The prince grew uncomfortable as he recalled Josephine telling him she was a traveling minstrel because he didn't believe she was the princess she claimed to be. Everything she said was true. Even her lie, was still true. He sighed, "Everyone adores her. Even those who have never met her. Makes me wonder if I'm just another admirer, who has mistaken it for love."

"Everyone loves to be admired. It is an exhilarating feeling. But for some, it is not enough to be loved by many. They must be loved by one." The old woman nodded. "*The* one. The princess, was not looking for love of many."

"But, so many love her. She has helped many people in so many ways. Loving her would only tie her down, cage her."

"She said 'yes' to you, no?"

"Yes!"

"Then, perhaps she is ready for a new life."

"How do I know for certain?"

The old woman felt a smirk snake across her face. "My boy, you ask her."

Prince Wendell laughed with her. They spoke long into the night. He had come here for a short rest from his travels. He never imagined it would also give him a rest from several other burdens as well. For the first time in a long while, he felt light and resolved. He was going to find Josephine and he was going to win her back.

Chapter 26

The Fool had managed to sneak away from his assistant after the young man had fallen asleep. His new assistant was all thanks to an order by the queen. She wanted to make sure he had plenty of help to ensure the success of his project.

"What better way to celebrate the union of Prince Wendell and Princess Olivia?" the queen had told him weeks ago.

The thought of the wedding made the fool nauseous. Nothing that had happened in the last few weeks made sense. Why is the prince marrying Princess Olivia after proposing to Josephine? Why has he left and where did he go? Of all the thoughtless things Wendell could have done. The prince was needed here more than ever. He resolved to give the prince a serious lashing as soon as he saw him again.

Until then, the best he could do was be here for Josephine. It had been too long since his last visit with her, thanks to his new assistant. Who was he kidding? He knew he was being guarded. It was obvious the very second he saw that look from Katerina, the queen. The moment when she learned he was working in the very same dungeons she had imprisoned Josephine in. The man wasn't even clever about hiding his new role. As soon as the Fool heard the young man say the word 'assistant' he wasted no time putting the infiltrator to work with meaningless tasks. As if he would actually trust the queen's lackey with details of his project, he may be *the* Fool of the castle but he wasn't *a* fool. He had worked the poor guard hard in the hopes he would fall asleep during one of his tasks. The Fool wanted him to have a nice long nap, so he had plenty of time to direct towards Josephine. The last thing he needed was to for her to lose hope.

He found his way to Princess's Josephine's door and peered in to say hello.

Instead, he said, "Love what you have done with the place!"

He couldn't help it. The first and only thing he could see clearly was a tower of mattresses. He had to squint to see the princess lounging at the very top.

The princess laughed. "I'm so glad you like it! But honestly I'm happier to see you."

After the Fool launched more water and peas over to her, she began to tell him how she was able to acquire the mattresses from the queen. Then she had to explain *why* she asked for mattresses in the first place, and then finally how she managed to get up to the top. It was all thanks to a few well-placed tugs, a push here and a pull there, which allowed Josephine to form some sort of stairway that allowed her to ascend to the top of her fluffy tower.

The fool was leaning comfortably against the other side of the princess's door. "I cannot believe she fell for the 'guide book' trick." Fool chuckled as he took a swig of water from his own container. "And now you have your bed, even if it is a bit extreme. How do you like it?"

"The view is nice," She chuckled. "I can see into the void of darkness much better now. Though, the mattresses are a bit lumpy for my taste."

The fool laughed so hard he choked on his water. "I'll send the complaints to your host."

When the laughter died down, Josephine started to talk in a slow and sincere voice. "My mother taught me that trick. One day I was arguing with my sisters; I can't even remember what it was about. She was so angry with me, but instead of yelling she asked me what The Royal's Guide to Etiquette said about arguing. When I didn't have an answer I was sent to the library to figure it out. I wasn't allowed to leave until I had found the book open to the page with the correct answer. She had me searching through shelves of books looking for this guide. After allowing me to struggle for hours, pouring over books on etiquette and demeanor she came in to ask me what I had found. I told her I found tons of information on etiquette and fighting and fighting etiquette, but I couldn't find The Royal's Guide to anything. Then she asked me what I learned. Just by looking through all those books, trying to find the answer to one simple question, I realized how ridiculous I had been acting. I told her how embarrassed I felt about my behavior. It was only after I apologized that my mother sat me down and told me there is no 'Royal's Guide to Etiquette', or anything for that matter. It is the job of a princess to process all the information I could find and formulate my own opinions. No one can tell you what to do, but when you have accepted your own opinion as fact it becomes a part of you."

"It is a good lesson, and a good trick."

"Yes. How do you know about it?"

"I've been around."

THE FOURTH PRINCESS

"So have I, and I've only seen my mother use it."

"Well..." Fool stuttered, "I've been around longer."

Josephine nodded as she fell silent in her cozy prison.

The fool felt terrible. He was there to cheer her up and he didn't seem to be doing a good job at the moment. With a sigh, he muttered something to himself.

"What did you say?" Josephine asked

"I said, I'm glad you were able to pull a trick on the queen."

"Once she realizes I outsmarted her, I'm afraid I'll be even higher on her list of people to hate."

"She doesn't hate you, she hates me."

"Excuse me?"

Fool panicked. How could he have slipped yet again? The harder he searched for a quick witted answer the more he realized he would have to tell the truth eventually.

The fool cleared his throat nervously. "Princess, I think it's time I told you the real reason the queen dislikes you."

"She thinks I'm not good enough for her son."

"Yes, but there's more to it. And it's kind of a long story"

"I could use a good story to occupy my time."

"When the king fell ill I was called in to help. I worked very closely with him and Katerina."

"Katerina?"

"My apologies, I meant to say the queen. The more her husband started to slip away, the more she leaned on me for support and encouragement. She began turning to me for everything, from the demands of the kingdom, to worries about her son. Eventually that constant need to be with me turned into love and she began to make up reasons to summon me, just so I could be close by. The only problem was, I did not love her. Not in the way she wanted me to, at least. She approached me one day to confess her feelings. I heard her out. But when she finished and expected me to respond in turn, all I could tell her was I did not feel the same.

"I explained to her that I had already given my love to another woman and could never love someone to that extent again. I had hoped she would understand, but matters of the heart are… complex. She became jealous and was determined to learn about this mystery woman I loved. Through means and contacts I still don't understand, she discovered my love's identity. The Queen also learned that she had married another man and had a family with him. Katerina was so eager to share this with me, perhaps in a last ditch hope of convincing me to love her in return. What she didn't know is that I already knew of the life my love had made and I was happy for her. That made Katerina even angrier. Now, she was embarrassed and upset because I had turned her down for a woman I could never have. Embarrassment became anger. Instead of simply sending me away, she took advantage of her husband's madness and joined him in laughing at everything I said. Eventually everyone in the castle was laughing as well.

"I wanted to leave, but my reputation as a doctor was tarnished. No one took me seriously anymore. Later the queen 'took pity' on me by offering a position here at the castle as the palace fool. I couldn't think of a better situation, so I stayed."

"And after all these years you still can't find anything better?" Josephine asked. "You're still playing her fool."

"I couldn't leave the prince. You've seen his relationship with his mother. Not much of that has changed. And when the king turned ill the prince distanced himself more and more from his father. He was no longer a comfort to the prince. So, without a father figure, Wendell turned to me. I felt if I left it would be too much for such a young boy to endure. Over the years he has grown on me. He feels like the son I never had. I cannot walk away from him until I know he is able to take his rightful place on the throne. So… I stay."

"That… is a monstrous story, Doctor." The princess sighed as she looked down at her pouch of peas. "Yes, staying for the prince is admirable, but she has you under her foot as some sick reminder of her control over you."

"It looks that way. However, from my perspective, I am a reminder to her that she does not always get what she wants."

"I suppose that makes me feel a little better. But how does this relate to me?"

There was a long pause before he spoke again.

"Because," The fool smiled sadly as he sighed. "Because my mystery woman is Queen Laurel, your mother."

Josephine blinked in silence as she thought. "My mother?"

"Yes."

"She's married. To my father."

"I know."

"They love each other. Very much!"

"I am aware of this, Princess."

"And you loved her!" She gasped. "You still love her!"

"Yes." The fool's voice was a soft, low whisper. The word barely carried over the cavern to Josephine's ears.

Chapter

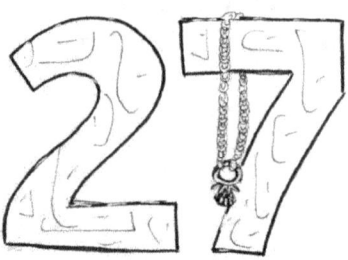

Several days passed since the fool had told Josephine of his past relationship with her mother, Queen Laurel. Fool was embarrassed to tell Josephine the truth, but she needed to know the entire story since the queen was punishing her for it. Finally, the fool was able to break free from his, so called, assistant so he could visit the princess again. He wasn't sure how well she would receive him, but he knew she must be hungry. After shooting over the pouches of water and peas, he filled her in on his latest success with his explosive project. When there was nothing else to talk about, the princess finally asked the question the fool had been waiting for.

"How do you know my mother?"

She was much more calm and controlled than a few days ago. The fool smiled as he drifted back into his memories. He settled himself into his spot against the locked door to the cave. Then, he took a few drinks of water and continued the story Josephine was invested in. She listened to each word as if they were sweet drops of honey she eagerly waited to lap up.

"We grew up together," Fool said. Feeling a bit more calm and confident, he continued. "My father was a brilliant man, a scholar that was fascinated by almost every subject. He was sought out by the king, your grandfather, and asked to be the private tutor for his little princess. In return, he would take care of food and housing and grant my father unlimited access to whatever he needed for proper instruction regarding his daughter. He accepted with one condition. My father wished to teach me alongside the princess. The king saw no issue with it, so as soon as we were settled in our new home, classes began.

"Laurel and I were always together learning new things, helping each other study, we were even allowed to play together occasionally. Time passed and we grew up. Laurel knew my strengths and weaknesses as well as I knew hers. Although, I can't seem to remember your mother having many weaknesses." The fool smiled to himself as the memories swept him away. "We fell in love. Neither of us expected it. We were both caught off guard. I knew she was off limits and she knew it was her duty to grow up to marry a prince. Our love complicated things."

"Complicated? If you loved each other enough wouldn't you have made it work?"

The fool took a deep breath. "Not with us. You see, your mother had the potential to be a skilled ruler. I could tell from the start she would grow into a loved but fair queen. To deny an entire generation of that wisdom and peace just so we could be together… it would be selfish. She would do the most good as the queen she was destined to be. I on the other hand was comfortable with machines and science. Understanding the mysteries of the human body fascinated me. My passion was for healing the sick and fixing things to function properly. Your mother understood that if I married her to become a king, I would be burdened by the pressures of ruling a kingdom instead of free to pursue these interests. She said it would be a tragedy if I were not free to serve the many people in need of my skills. Not many others are as talented in these matters as I am. She believed I was pioneering new solutions to complex medical issues beyond the study experts were doing at the time. Because we loved each other very much, we encouraged each other to follow our destinies apart. No matter how much our hearts ached to be together, we knew we would live a lifetime of regret not pursuing our callings.

"Once we accepted the logic to all of this, Laurel and I made a vow that we would never forget each other as we flourished in the lives we chose. To do otherwise… our sacrifices would have been in vain. We even exchanged tokens to remember our vow to each other and to ourselves… that was the last time I saw her."

"Fool, this is a terrible story. It's not right that you would deny yourselves a life of true happiness because of your so called destinies. It sounds absolutely ridiculous. How do you know that's how destiny works? How do you know it wasn't your destiny to marry each other and live happily ever after?"

"Who knows anymore? It happened so long ago whatever future we might have had is long gone. This is the destiny we agreed upon. I've tried to move on, knowing that she would have to do the same, for the sake of her inheritance. My problem is there is no one who could ever compare to Laurel."

"And I was hoping for a good story to possibly cheer up this gloomy prison."

He laughed at the irony, "You're right, I am probably the worst fool ever." Fool could hear her chuckle bounce off the walls inside. Her laugh always put a spring back in his step.

"If you don't mind me asking, what were your tokens?"

"Laurel gave me her favorite jeweled comb. I still have it safely tucked away with my things. I gave her my family's ring. It had been passed down from father to son for generations. It is the same ring you wear around your neck."

Josephine instantly touched the ring tucked away beneath her blouse. "Mother had given all my sisters, and me, a special piece of jewelry before we left home. I remember admiring each piece, as she gave them away, so beautiful, so special. When I told her I was leaving my gift was this ring. I tried not to show it on my face but I was disappointed. As if I didn't deserve one of her more elaborate and attractive pieces. She even told me it was one of her most cherished possessions and I should wear it as a reminder to never let anything stand in the way of my true destiny. I thought she made the whole thing up because it didn't look like something she cherished, nor did I understand how a ring was going to help me live up to my destiny. I felt she was disappointed in me, and she didn't feel I was worthy of owning something more beautiful. Now I understand how important this ring is. I understand her love for me, and the love she must have felt for you. It must have been a terrible sacrifice. However, from what I have seen, you both have remained true to your vow."

"Thank you princess." The fool smiled. "And you have to know that if she could see the woman you have grown into, and I have come to admire, she would be bursting with pride."

Tears welled up in Josephine's eyes as she fingered the ring. "I hope so…" She whispered.

Chapter

Several kingdoms away, Prince Wendell pulled a clean shirt over his freshly washed body. King Fauntleroy had sent an escort out to meet up with him near the border, and bring him to the castle immediately. The king was eager to meet up with him and talk, but not eager enough that Wendell couldn't have a good cleaning first. The Prince remembered the king from when he was a little boy. He was a passionate man, always laughing, and always the center of attention. The prince remembered being scared of King Fauntleroy at first until he saw how comfortable his father was around him. The two kings were forever friends and as such King Fauntleroy became a familiar figure in the castle. Of course, Wendell had not seen King Fauntleroy since his father became sick. His mother didn't want anyone to know he was having problems. This meant no more visitors, no more parties, and no more fun. At least he had the Fool to keep his spirits up, and then came Princess Josephine. He had to find her. He could not allow his father's castle to fall into such a gloomy, reclusive state again. How and why he had endured that atmosphere was a mystery to him, and he would not return to that life. He pulled on his jacket then headed down to the throne room.

The prince bowed low before the king showing as much respect and honor as he could.

"Prince Wendell of Tridith! There's no need to be so formal, boy! Your father and I were good friends."

The prince smiled as he straightened up. "Your highness, I thank you for your hospitality."

The king bounced down the stairs nearly falling on top of the prince as he gave him a bone crushing embrace.

"My goodness boy you have grown into a man! What a special treat this is. You look so much like your father, only much better looking. You know, your father could never compare to my dashing looks!"

The prince laughed, "Thank you."

The king led him over to a set of chairs to sit in while they talked. "When I heard reports of you nearby I knew I needed to arrange a meeting. I was not going to let you pass though my kingdom without a hot meal, and good company at the very least. And then the news of your engagement... I feel like throwing a party in your honor!"

The prince's eyes popped, "You know of my engagement?"

"Of course I do, my boy! We received a formal notice a few weeks ago from your mother, Queen Katerina. Usually notices aren't sent until a wedding date is set, but who cares. Your mother deserves the chance to dote on her only son. Don't be embarrassed by her."

"I'm surprised actually. Last I heard she wasn't fond of the woman I wanted to marry."

"Well the notice sounded pretty exciting. She's promising a spectacle on your behalf guaranteed to astound everyone who attends."

"Wow that does sound exciting, but we kind of need a bride for there to be a wedding. That's why I'm here. I've been looking for her."

"Why isn't she with you?"

"It's complicated."

"Was she stolen from you?"

"No, she left."

"Women!" The king sat down in his chair. "Well you're doing the right thing. All women act crazy before they get married. This is probably some game she's playing to make sure you chase after her. They like to see those kind of displays of love."

"You think she left to see if I would chase her?"

"I don't know, I just know women can be crazy."

The prince shook his head a little, "Well if I do find her, and win her back then of course you must come to the wedding."

"Absolutely! I'd hate to think how boring and drab your big day would be without me there with you."

"Indeed, it would be absolutely terrible." Wendell answered with a smile.

There was a pause as King Fauntleroy leaned forward in his chair towards the prince.

"So, what news of your father? I haven't heard from him in years and I thought something dreadful might have happened to him."

The prince wasn't sure what to say. "Um, no, he is just fine. Nothing dreadful happening to him. My father, he… he's sick."

The king's eye's narrowed. "That's an awful long time for someone to be sick."

Wendell nodded, "Yes, your highness, it is."

They stared at each other, trying to read one another's thoughts.

"Are you sure your father is not dead?"

"Yes, I am sure he's not dead." The prince rolled his eyes.

"Missing then?"

"Definitely not missing. Just… sick."

"You know, I used to know this doctor by the name of Kendell Krouss. He was brilliant when it came to illnesses. I'm not sure where he is now, but I'm certain we could find him to help out with whatever you father has."

The prince chose his words carefully. He didn't want to betray the family secret concerning his father. The last thing he wanted was to hear of his father's glorious legacy smeared all because he went mad in the end. At the same time, King Fauntleroy deserved to know why his friend hasn't talked to him in all these years.

"I'm afraid, there are some things even the great Doctor Krouss cannot cure. Even if he had half a lifetime."

The king looked deep into Wendell's eyes. The seriousness of his face combined with the looming silence unnerved the prince. Finally, the king spoke. "Who has been running things?"

"King Theodore, my father." The answer came so abrupt and scripted that the king immediately asked the question again.

"Who has been running things?" This time his arms were crossed and he glared at the prince, daring him to lie a second time.

"My mother…" The prince was about to lie again, but immediately changed his mind. Josephine would never want to marry a liar. "… Believes she's in charge, but in the end it's me. I've been running the kingdom."

The king noticeably relaxed, and a proud smile formed on his lips. "You have grown into a fine young man. Your father would be proud." The prince nodded his appreciation. "In lieu of this new information I suggest we skip the engagement party and send you home right away."

The prince didn't expect the king to say something like that to him. "Excuse me?"

"If your father is sick, and you are out chasing after this princess then that means Katerina is running things back home. We cannot allow that to happen. You must go home, now."

"But what about…"

"Send trusted messengers out to find her instead. You're mother cannot handle Tridith on her own. She does not know how."

"Wait a minute, how do you know…"

"It's not important, you cannot be away right now. It's time for you to put your foot down and take your place as king, with or without Olivia."

"Olivia?"

"Princess Olivia, the woman you're searching for. The woman you're going to marry?" The king saw the prince's demeanor darken in an instant. "You're not searching for Princess Olivia, are you?"

The wheels turned noisily in Wendell's mind. Had he been a machine the whining, deafening strain and grinding speed would be sure to terrify anyone nearby. Rage bubbled up in his chest and a menacing fire sparked in his eyes. The prince took a deep breath to compose himself.

"Thank you for your hospitality, but you're right, I should be returning home… immediately."

The king looked worried, the same look Wendell's father had when he found the prince fretting too much over a mistake he had made.

"Hold on, my boy." King Fauntleroy put a hand on Wendell's shoulder to keep him seated. "Who are you looking for?"

THE FOURTH PRINCESS

"Josephine. I will be marrying Princess Josephine."

Now it was the king's turn to squirm under the intense glare the prince gave him.

"Princess Josephine of Ebren?"

"You know her? Have you seen her?"

The king shifted uncomfortably. "I have never met her, but I hear her stories being told all around my kingdom."

"Yes, I am just now becoming familiar with a few of these stories of her. I am starting to realize how much I underestimated her while she was my guest."

"Surely you know, not all are true; and her actions are not as miraculous as they say."

"Of course, but in each story lies a foundation of truth. One small deed by someone can be seen as a miracle to another."

"A dangerous misconception, to make someone out to be more than what they really are."

"And who do you believe Princess Josephine to be?"

"What I know is she is the youngest of four sisters, with nothing extraordinary to offer other than her birthright. She grew tired of living in the shadow of her family, so she left. Now she appears randomly in various places to establish a name for herself, hoping to validate her existence in this world."

At first the prince was angry. King Fauntleroy, a man who has never met the princess, had no right to dismiss her so easily. But he could not contradict anything the King had said. Princess Josephine always spoke of her family with adoration, as if they could do no wrong. She had no kingdom to inherit. All the princess had was her name, Princess Josephine Helena Carmina of Ebren, the youngest daughter of King Ronald and Queen Laurel. Even that name she shied away from; going by the nickname Four. Her formal title hung heavily around her neck as a constant reminder of her place in the world. Perhaps she did need some validation. Anything to know she was more than just her name. She needed to see there was something special about her, and only her.

The prince immediately felt embarrassed. He had always assumed Josephine to be a confident, self-satisfied woman. In his mind she was someone who didn't care about the opinions of others to follow her own heart. The truth was, in one aspect, she was just like every other princess he met. She was a frail porcelain doll, easily chipped and broken. The Princess was so ready to give comfort or help to those around her, but no one… not even he, could see she needed just as much help.

"There is truth to what you say," Prince Wendell began. "I believe she is a woman with many hidden struggles she must face every day, but I do not agree when you say she has nothing extraordinary to offer."

"Does she really have anything of value to offer when she is constantly distressed by the opinions of others?"

"Your Highness, the pain is what gives her strength. Without it, there would be no reason for her to try to become better. The more she helps, the more she learns, the better princess she becomes. A princess that the people already respect and love."

"But will that ever be enough for her?"

The prince smiled a knowing smile, "No, it won't."

The king blinked in surprise, "No?"

"More often than not, it isn't the love of many that we desire. It usually is the love of a few or the one. All Princess Josephine wants is to know that she is worthy of her family's legacy. She needs to know that she belongs with them." He paused for a moment to reflect his own feelings. "It is the same with me, only I wish to be worthy of her. All the love in the world doesn't matter if it is not from the one you care about the most."

The king had a proud smile on his face as he listened to the prince. This was no mere prince he was sitting with. This was a powerful man with all the knowledge and confidence of a king.

"I should like to meet this Josephine, if she is all that you say. I will find her for you, so you can return home promptly. Tell me where you saw her last."

"Well, we were at the castle. She went for a stroll with my mother, and then..." The prince's calm dwindled with every passing second. He couldn't believe how blind he had been as the truth crashed down on him like bricks. His rage boiled up again as his fists clinched and eyes flashed.

"...and then?" inquired the king.

The prince looked up, his face as unyielding and unforgiving as stone. "Thank you for your help, but I think I can handle things now. You're right, I should be getting home... immediately."

He got up before King Fauntleroy could even dismiss him properly. The king didn't care, he seemed to be reading Prince Wendell's mind as he kept steady pace with him all the way to the door where the prince's horse was waiting for him.

"God speed on your journey, Prince Wendell. Keep me informed if you require *anything*."

The prince nodded and bowed elegantly to the king.

"Again, thank you for everything your highness."

Wendell couldn't get on his horse fast enough. The prince felt like such a fool. He needed to be home... now, but he still had a long journey back. All he could do was press on as fast as he could. Finding the princess was all that mattered, and now he knew exactly where she was.

Chapter 29

Josephine lay helplessly on top of her mattress tower. It had been a while since her friend, the Fool, had been able to sneak a visit, so she started conserving her peas. They were tucked away under the bottom mattress, so she wouldn't be tempted to eat them all at once. This was one of the few times where the phrase "out of sight, out of mind" was a blessing to her. The princess was rolling a stone in between her fingers. It was something to do with her hands while her mind meandered from one thought to the next. Everything had slowed down in the cave with no distractions to mix things up. Her movements, her breathing, a faint breeze from the cave, each had all the time in the world. She tried to sing but the tune was slow as well. Worse was the hollow echo of each note. The sounds crowding on top of another allowing the cave to feel vaster than it originally felt in the deadening silence.

THE FOURTH PRINCESS

Her spirits were dwindling. No news of the prince; no hope of rescue. Josephine's strength was fading. All she had to keep her company were her own thoughts. She thought of Prince Wendell and how happy they were together. She thought of her sisters, each one in turn. Why not? She had the time. Each sister should be able to occupy her mind without fear of being bundled up into a group. She thought of her father, and the lessons he taught. She thought of her mother, her kindness and love. The more she thought about her mother, the more she thought of the doctor, Fool, her friend.

His story saddened her. She would want her mother to be with the man she loved; although, she couldn't imagine her being with anyone other than her father. Does she even love him? Does she still love the doctor the way he loves her still? The Fool claimed to be happy and proud of his life. As for her, all she could feel was torment. She knew she would never have the courage to sacrifice her heart's desire the way her mother did. Did that make her unworthy of being a princess? Would she ever be able to do the right thing for her kingdom? These questions always started a disturbing spiral of worries that sent her plummeting into self-doubt. She would try to break away by focusing on the happier memories, but the questions would always intrude like an unwelcome guest.

"Will I ever be enough?" She whispered.

The question unhinged her for a moment, long enough for her to lose control of the stone in her hands. She listened as it fell. She heard a loud crack as it hit the stone platform below her followed by a steady rumble as it rolled and then, silence. Josephine closed her eyes as a single tear formed on her lashes, and creeped ever so smoothly behind her ear and into her hair.

Splash! The sound startled the princess as her eyes snapped open. It wasn't loud, but in the silence of the cave it might as well had been a fanfare of trumpets. Calmly... carefully... she climbed down from her tower of mattresses to the stone platform.

The princess peeked over the edge, and was unsurprised by the impending darkness that was always there, as constant as ever. She took a small knife from her pocket and cut open a corner on one of the mattresses. In no time she had a large bundle of feathers, straw and other things used for stuffing that she cared little about. She grabbed some nearby stones and started striking them together. With time and a generous portion of patience, she managed to make a few sparks. One spark fell onto the pile of fluff setting it ablaze. She bundled more stuffing from her mattress into one of the empty pouches Fool had shot over to her and tightened the chord on top. Then she lit it on fire. Quickly she dropped it over the edge to watch it fall. Down, down, down it went giving off an orange hue until the light simply winked out. It had hit water.

A faint breeze ticked her nose again. This time she was focused and she recognized something new. The breeze was salty. The princess remembered the castle being set up near a sharp cliff that dropped into the sea. She must be somewhere inside a cave in that cliff, probably carved out naturally by the water over time. In lieu of this new information an entirely new list of questions formed. Questions she didn't mind entertaining. She welcomed each one eagerly. How deep is the water? Would there be an opening big enough for her to escape to the sea? Would it be entirely underwater? She sorted through each question with the facts she now knew.

"The water below must be linked to the tides," she concluded. However, was it high tide or low tide? Was it coming in or going out? More questions, but these could be answered in time. Her mind and body was awakened from the nothing-ness that had started to consume her. Josephine had a project, and then there would be a plan. She was getting out of here, even if she had to arrange it herself. A familiar feeling enveloped her as she worked out what to do next. It was a feeling she had always taken for granted but now burned inside her with a passion; she felt hope.

Chapter

It took almost a week before the prince was able to set eyes on his kingdom again. He and his horse had ridden hard, anxious to get home. When he reached the first village all he could hear was talk about the upcoming wedding for Prince Wendell and the Princess Olivia. The buzzing of gossip grew from a small hum to an uproar the closer he rode to the castle. When he finally saw his home towering off in the distance there was a bitter taste in his mouth. Talk of the wedding only confirmed what he had suspected. His mother was behind all this mayhem. He had no doubt that she already knew where Josephine was. She set this wedding up in his absence. Once again she was up to her own devices without any regard for his opinion. She has been on her own agenda for too long and it was time for him to end it.

Wendell needed to figure out exactly how he was going to take over his kingdom, as King Fauntleroy insisted. He had no proof that she had a maniacal plan falling seamlessly into place. Accusations alone would not convince the queen to come clean about the princess either. If he approached her now, he would be playing right into her hands. He needed a plan. He needed to think. Sadly, all of his best thoughts were hatched in the most comfortable room in the castle… Fool's room. He knew he couldn't go there, he would be spotted for sure and his mother notified. Not nearly enough time to sort out a proper strategy. He thought about where Josephine would go. Immediately he remembered the tavern they had visited, but quickly dismissed the idea. He needed to hide.

A salty wind caressed his brow turning his eyes to the sea. The cool air felt welcoming after riding so long. An odd sense of peace washed over him as he directed his horse toward a path that skirted the edge of the cliff face. He dismounted and walked alongside his horse for a bit, to allow the animal some rest. The path wound its way back behind the castle soon enough. It was a place hardly anyone ventured due to the angry bursts of wind that accompany the waves as the tide rushed in. But now, the tide was heading out, so it was a nice place to lay low and find some rest.

The cliff was an excellent place to think and work out a plan. Perhaps, a bit too good of a place because the Prince's thoughts and worries crashed on him like the waves on the rocks below. He felt so naive for allowing his mother so much control over his life. He felt equal to every haughty royal he had always hated for believing they were too good to be around their inferiors. He had treated Josephine the same way and despised himself for it. Furthermore, he felt even lower after he had left his kingdom to look for her. So many people knew of The Fourth Princess. There were so many stores of her kindness. Each story was a constant testament of her unselfishness and love. Who was he compared to Josephine? What has *he* done to deserve someone as remarkable as her?

For the first time in years he took the time to think of his father. He longed for a world where his father wasn't so ill. If he was of sound mind all would be different; perhaps even better. His father would know what to do. He would be the one to work this out. He would know exactly how to confront the queen without crumbling under her pressure.

And yet, among all the negativity that bore down on him at that moment, his heart still flipped when he thought about Josephine. For reasons the prince couldn't fathom, she had chosen to be with him. She had said 'yes' to his proposal. There must be something about him, something uniquely special that would attract such an extraordinary woman. A true princess, regardless of lineage. How he yearned to be with her. He needed her by his side, now more than ever. Nothing felt right. Nothing made sense. His world was upside down, and he knew only she could help set it right. A kaleidoscope of emotions frothed up to his chest as he shouted with all his capacity towards the sea, releasing all his energies in one word.

"Josephine!"

He fell to his knees unable to stand and too weak to care. Before he could stop them, tears began to flood. Unable to think of anything better to do; he remained still, and allowed each tear to fall.

Chapter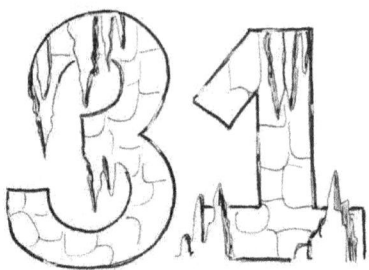

Josephine looked up into the empty void of her cave. She heard something. It was muffed and jumbled from the echoes of the cave, but she could have sworn she heard her name. The odd part was the sound came from inside the cave, not the door that led up towards the prisons. Why would someone be calling her from over there?

"Unless..." She spoke out loud to jolt her out of her thoughts. The princess took a futile glace over the platform. There was still nothing to see, but she imagined how deep the water had gotten over the past few days. She had been tossing stones gauging distance as best as she could. It was definitely deeper, except for the last few days. The tide was going out. Was it deep enough?

"Enough questions." Josephine told herself. That *was* her name she heard. If she was waiting for a sign, that was it. The princess hesitated for a moment. She didn't want to simply leap to her doom hoping she would survive. She frantically searched around at what she had. Rocks, peas, a mattress… no, twelve mattresses. She crouched down to grab hold of the bottom of the tower and jerked with all her strength. Little by little the tower pulled away from the wall. She couldn't believe how a fluffy little mattress could amass so much weight when piled on top of many others.

"No matter, the more weight the better," she thought as she wiggled around to the wall and started to push from the other side with her legs. The tower wavered from side to side. The princess took a calming breath to stifle her excitement. She needed the mattress tower intact until the last possible moment. Today was the first day she was grateful for the miniscule size of the platform. It did not take her long to maneuver the pillar to the edge. She stood for a second, to collect whatever strength she had left. Then, in an instant, she sprang off the wall into a short sprint and tackled the bottom mattresses head on. The sudden force shook the tower as it slid into the empty void. Josephine recoiled a bit to keep from going over the edge with the mattresses, then jumped on the topmost mattress just as it fell past the platform.

Wind rushed past her ears as she tried to get a tight hold of the mattress. Beneath her she could hear the slap of the beds as each hit the water. The lower mattresses helped to break her fall as she landed on a few others. The jolt still took her by surprise. Icy, cold water smashed in her face as her mattress skimmed the surface of the water. She clung on for dear life as she was swept away by the current. It would have been a nice ride, had it not been for crashing waves constantly soaking her with water. The current was drawn to the stone outcrops swirling around each one in a rush which dragged the princess along with it. Bruised and surely bleeding, she hung on; awaiting the end to this fearsome battle between the forces of nature. The corner of her eye glimpsed something as she struggled for a breath between rushes of water… Sunlight!

Her heart leapt. "Just a little longer," she repeated to herself while scrambling to tighten her already white knuckle grip on her raft.

Chapter

The Prince rubbed his head in his hands. The tears had stopped and all he could do was stare out into the sea. He took in the majestic beauty of his surroundings. The feel of the wind, seagulls hovering in the air, the crash of the waves against the glistening rocks.

His eyes drifted down to the blue waters carrying mattresses out to sea.

"Mattresses?" Wendell wondered. He stood over by the cliff edge to get a better look.

Sure enough several mattresses had appeared in the water from somewhere inside the cliff. He made his way down the side of the edge to get a better look. With all the pressing issues on his mind, investigating an odd appearance of mattresses was an inviting distraction. *There,* he could see a small entrance into the cliff where water would rush in and just as quickly spill out while dragging soggy beds along with it. There were so many of them, but there was only one his eyes fixed upon. This one held a person on it, scrambling to stay above water. He rushed further down the cliff to help.

His eyes remained locked on the person as they were tossed by the waves like a rag doll. He had climbed as far down as he could and paused to determine what to do next. The frail, half drowned figure was clearer now. His heart stopped for an instant as he recognized her.

"Josephine!" He shouted, and without further thought dove into the waters to reach her.

Not the best idea, he thought as the tides proceeded to drag him two and fro. He pressed on, swimming as hard as possible toward the princess. After what felt like an eternity of fighting the currents, he managed to break from the water with the princess and onto the dry rocks to safety.

"Josephine?" he whispered. He sat her upright, smacking her back to rid her lungs of any water. She sputtered then gasped for air.

Her eyes lazily opened to see Prince Wendell's face next to hers, holding her close. He stroked her hair off of her face, then held onto her hand.

"Wendell!" Her hand tightened onto his, yet another thing she was unwilling to let go of. She smiled, "It was you."

"It is me, Josephine. I'm here."

She wasn't listening to him. "It was you calling for me!"

He watched her smile grow with every breath. Her heart slowed to a normal speed, and her muscles relaxed a bit. Wendell allowed her to remain slumped in his arms while he caressed her face with his fingers. She finally, sat up and shook the water from her hair. What was once terror and panic on her face, had now melted away to reveal her usual smooth confidence.

"It was nice of you to show up." She spoke as a smile curved her lips and her eyes narrowed on him.

The prince relaxed. He knew she was back to her old self.

"Well, you know, I knew you could handle yourself." He teased.

Her eyes grew wide as he teased her in turn. "Would you like to know exactly what I've been handling while you have been… who knows where?" Her tone balanced delicately between yelling and lecturing.

"I've been off looking for you! I was told you didn't want to be cooped up in a palace for the rest of your life, so you decided to run away."

"Who gave you that preposterous idea?" She demanded.

The prince stared at her not wanting to answer. The frustration that stained his face read loud and clear to Josephine. She knew exactly who would lie to him like that.

She sputtered in disbelief, "And, you believed her?"

"Look, I've been second guessing everything I've ever known since I left the kingdom looking for you. I don't need you tormenting me any more than I already am."

The princess blinked at him. "You left the kingdom?"

"Looking for you, yes."

"*You*, got on your horse, and actually crossed your border into another kingdom?"

The prince was exasperated, "Yes, I went to a few actually. See I thought you would go west because…" His voice trailed off when she leaned over to kiss his lips. His shoulders relaxed as he pulled her even closer to him, refusing to let go.

"How did it feel?"

The prince was in a trance. "It felt great!"

Josephine smiled as she shook her head. "I meant about leaving your comfortable palace for a change."

Prince Wendell focused again. "Oh, yes, it felt good. It was an eye opener. I also learned more about you than I ever thought possible."

"Really?" The princess sounded doubtful.

"But, I learned nothing that would explain finding you here riding a mattress out to sea."

"It seemed like a smart idea at the time." She laughed when it struck her just how crazy the thought was, and how lucky she was he was near.

"You could have drowned."

"But I didn't"

"If I wasn't here…" the prince couldn't finish his sentence.

It bothered him that her life was in danger. It was even more disturbing that he was here to save her only by a mere coincidence.

"You *were* here." She turned his head so he could see into her eyes. "I only jumped because I heard my name. It was shouted at me though the caves. That was you, wasn't it?"

He nodded, not wanting to relive his moment of weakness.

The princess simply said, "When I needed you most, you were here."

He pulled her into his arms again. The thought of losing her threatened to slice at him. There were too many coincidences; too much left to chance. He swore to himself on those rocks he would never allow this to happen again. He would always be there for her, not just when it mattered, always.

Chapter

The Fool had just finished a routine check-up with the king. The queen had insisted Fool take on his role as doctor to see if her husband would be well enough to make an appearance at the prince's upcoming wedding. The Fool had already known the king would be able to handle the event; he enjoyed visiting the king from time to time. The fool used the Queen's order as an excuse to leave the looming eyes of his escort.

As he strolled down the hall leading away from the king's quarters, he passed a large window that overlooked the sea. It wasn't anything special other than a strategically placed window to allow more light in the castle. The view never changed either. Every time you would pass by you would see a large green meadow that gradually faded into the dark grey rocks of a sharp cliff. The waves would crash up every once in a while, but the cliff was so high all one could see was the water and the meadow. Except for today. The Fool actually saw a horse in the meadow. He paused to appreciate the change of scenery, even if it was just a stray horse. The Fool pressed his face up to the glass. That wasn't a stray horse, it was Prince Wendell's horse. Quickly he scanned the meadow as best as he could to find the prince as well.

"If his horse is here then he *must* be close by." He wanted to run outside to find the prince right away, but he decided to deliver the good news to the princess first. Helping her keep her wits was more important.

He raced through the hallways and down the stairs, through the gardens and along the hidden paths leading to the dungeons. He flew down the stairs racing deeper and deeper into the caves. The Fool spun around the corner to Princess Josephine's door and found himself nose to nose with Queen Katerina. The look on her face startled him so much he eagerly stepped back and bowed low to the queen to avoid her glare. The door to the princesses' solitude was open and several guards were investigating the cavern with torches. The tower of mattresses was gone save one lonely mat that clung onto the platform. The other thing missing; the princess.

"Fool!" The queen wasn't surprised, she was enraged. "What are you doing here?"

The fool was stunned. He was caught so off guard he barely was able to speak.

"I... was... coming to the caves, your majesty. I needed to practice more."

"Where are your supplies?" she asked coldly.

The fool suspected she knew the truth of why he was there, so he remained silent. A guard came up to the Queen and bowed before he spoke.

"Your Majesty, our torches are not bright enough to see the bottom of the pit. If she is down there, alive or dead, we are unable to see her. We did find these underneath the mattress on the platform though." He handed her two pouches, one water tight with a stopper plugged in the top and another filled with dried peas.

"The Princess is alive. Do not stop looking for her." She turned to look at the Fool still crouched on the floor, keeping silent. She leaned over and cupped the fool's face in her hands tenderly. Her voice was soft.

"After all I have done for you, all I have offered, you still insist on defying me?"

Her eyes took on a menacing, evil gaze.

The Fool tried to stare back defiantly, but it was no use. For the first time in his life, Doctor Kendell Krouss was terrified of the queen.

Chapter 34

"What should we do now?" Josephine asked as she rubbed her face with her hands.

The prince shook his head. "It's no use, I keep drawing a blank with my mother. I wish we could just run away and start over on our own terms."

"You wouldn't be able to do that. It would tear you to pieces leaving everything in her hands while knowing you should be here instead."

"Oh, but that's something *you* can do no problem." He meant to tease her, just to see her smile. Instead, her face turned solemn as she looked out to the sea.

"I already ran away, and I've been running every day since. Now I don't think I could go back, even if I wanted to." She locked eyes with him. "You would not want that life."

The prince immediately regretted his words. He still didn't understand how heavy of a burden her family had grown for her. No, not a burden, a standard. One that she didn't feel she could obtain. He squeezed her hand in support. He couldn't imagine what more she felt she needed to prove. In his opinion, if her family knew a fraction of what their little princess has been up to, they would rejoice to have her home again. He didn't think she had anything to worry about, but getting Josephine to believe it was another matter.

"Then tell me," he refocused the conversation back on the current problem. "If your mother had gone a bit crazy by dominating your life to the point of servitude, who would you turn to for help?"

Without hesitation Josephine answered, "My father." The prince blinked at her causing Josephine to feel guilty as she started to apologize. He knew she was only telling the truth, but it was not necessarily the best answer to give him. The prince gave her a small smirk with a shrug to show her he was alright.

"What would your father say to you then?"

"Say?" The question rattled her a bit as she reflected on it for a moment. She shook her head before she spoke, not liking the answer she came to. "He would remind me that she is my mother and his lovely wife. He loves her more than anything in the world, and she must have had a good reason for whatever she did."

Wendell's jaw fell open, "That's no help at all!"

"I'm sorry! That's what he would say!" Josephine yelled back defensively. "I'm just as lost as you are in this matter."

"You're telling me, he would take her side?"

She nodded her head. "Always. I remember it would bother me every time I would go and talk to him about something that had happened." She started to think again, then rolled her eyes in more frustration. "Except, he was always right."

"Excuse me?"

"He was always right. She would have a good reason for whatever she did. I just couldn't see it right away. And because he loves her, he trusts her reasoning as well. He wouldn't undermine her authority as my mother because I cry about it to him. She came first and foremost, and that wasn't going to change for anyone."

The prince spoke slowly to make sure he understood correctly. "Are you saying my mother is right?"

"I'm saying she must have a good reason to justify all of her actions to herself."

"Too bad she would never tell us what that reason is."

The princess tapped her lips in thought. "Maybe, someone else could."

"Who?"

"Your father."

The prince rolled his eyes as she tried to reason with him.

"Think about it," Josephine explained. "Is there anyone else who loves her so much they would immediately understand her logic behind all this? Anyone else who would be able to see things from her perspective?"

"Josephine, yes, he would be the one to ask. But, he cannot even form a thought in his mind. And, if he could, how would he communicate it?"

The princess sat calmly while he protested. "What other choice do we have?"

Wendell stared at her not wanting to speak. There had to be something else they could do, someone else to talk to. There wasn't. She was right. Wendell did not want to see his father. The king was such a fragile man; and the prince didn't want to strain his father with too much, or anything at all. Josephine waited patiently for him to say something. All he could feel was anxiety. The weight of what must be done settled heavily on his shoulders. He finally consented, but still with a painful, sick worry that he may destroy what little of a father he had left.

Chapter 35

The prince walked through the castle without a word. He wished there was anyone else they could turn to for help. He had a great amount of love for his father. Wendell could remember so many fond memories of them together, and the lessons he had been taught. They were close. But then the king's mind began to fade. He started to forget more with each passing day. Speaking and writing became a chore for him. His mother insisted on keeping the prince away from his father, so the doctors could have plenty of room for their work. Wendell felt his father had died a long time ago. Sure, the king was alive and well and would come out of his room for occasional appearances, only Wendell no longer saw him as his father. He was thinner, more fragile and much graver. If he spoke it was only a few words and he hardly ever made sense. However, the worst part was the look in his eyes. Whenever Wendell would look into them they felt empty, as if he was a hollow shell of his former great self. His eyes, usually vacant, would look straight through the prince as if he wasn't even there. The king was merely an old faded copy of his former self.

For as much distance the prince tried to fit between them there was still one problem; he loved the king more than anything. He would find himself wishing his father was well, so things could be as they were, content and exciting. The more he wished the more pain he felt, due to the harsh reality. He didn't want to face the pain. He knew once he saw his father all the memories would flood back. All the love and hope would swell up in his chest as it always did allowing the prince a moment of joy. A moment of perfect joy which would turn into a terrible tease as it all splintered away the second his father would try to do something. A harsh reminder that even though they were inches away his father was no longer with him.

The prince stared at the door to the king's chamber. *How did we get here so quickly?* He thought as he tried to find the strength to knock. Josephine stood behind him silent as she waited patiently for his next move.

"You know, he may not even recognize me, or anyone for that matter. This could be one grand waste of time."

Josephine looked back at him calmly, un-phased by his protest. "Or…"

The prince closed his eyes as he lifted his hand and knocked. A small server opened the door and bowed low when he saw it was the prince.

"Your highness! How may I serve you?"

The prince cleared his throat to allow a little more confidence in his words. "I'm here to seek council from my father." The server looked unsure. "Is there a problem?

"Oh, not at all Prince Wendell. I was just told by the queen not to have the king bothered by anyone until after the wedding."

A bother? The servant thought he would be a bother to his own father? He would have gotten angry at the poor little man, were it not for a small voice in his head reminding himself that was exactly what he thought he was doing, bothering his father.

"Sir, are you seriously considering denying me an audience with my own father?"

The man panicked a little as beads of sweat formed on his brow. "Of course not your highness." He fumbled into another bow. "Yes, of course, do come in. If you need anything I will be just outside the door."

Josephine and the prince entered as the doors closed behind them. The room itself was an unexpected surprise. There was a bed, dressers and shelves, but in every other nook and cranny were paintings. Some paintings were hung on the walls with care, others were stretched and stacked on the floor. There were rolled paintings, framed paintings, and unfinished paintings. There were some on easels, others on desks, even on the bed. The dark stone walls had been painted as well. The king sat on a stool in front of a large easel. In his hand were a few brushes he held in a manner in which a flick of the wrist, could alternate to whichever brush suited him. Each picture was painted in their own unique style, but all were of the same beautiful, green landscape. All in all, the room was cheerful, giving the effect the occupants were standing by a lovely countryside instead of a stony palace chamber.

The prince didn't care much about the room's décor. He could not take his eyes from the king. Prince Wendell could not remember the last time his father looked so focused. He wanted to entertain the idea that King Theodore may be getting better. Immediately he snuffed it out, not wanting to dwell on false hope. As he drew closer, the prince announced himself and bowed.

"Father? It's me, Wendell. I was hoping to talk to you for a bit."

The king froze in mid stroke with his brush and looked up at the prince. He cocked his head to one side and stayed there for a moment eyeing him. Wendell looked at Josephine for help, who looked back at him just as unsure. Before the prince could say any more there was a clatter of brushes dropping to the floor where the king dropped them. As fast as lightening King Theodore had risen from his stool and scooped his son up in his arms.

Chapter 36

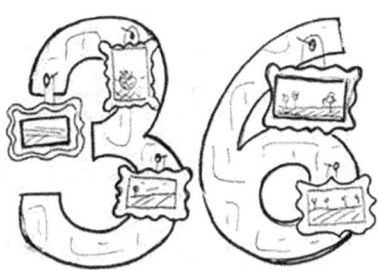

Prince Wendell and the king stood there for a while, simply holding each other in a long, overdue embrace. The prince was a wash of emotions because of this one, unexpected surprise. He fought each one as hard as he could, still refusing to give in to his hopes. He didn't want to lose control and cry in front of his father. The king finally let go and took a step back to look at his son, and then he spoke.

"I like strawberries." His smile was so warm, so genuine, the prince caught his breath for a moment. He could not believe what was happening. Wendell's strong resolve waivered as he allowed a bright beaming smile to form on his face in return.

"Yes, I've heard that recently."

The king patted him on the cheek then looked over at Josephine with the same cocked head and burrowing eyes.

"Father, please allow me to introduce Princess Josephine of Ebren. She and I are planning to be married soon." The king still didn't move. Prince Wendell's worries started to tug at the back of his mind again. "I love her very much and asked her to stay here, as my wife, and she has accepted."

Unlike with the prince, the king slowly inched his way toward the princess. Although slow, he walked upright and confident. A shadow of the power he used to have engulfed him as he approached. Wendell and Josephine were elated to see a small glimpse of the real man behind his madness. The king tenderly scooped up Princess Josephine's hand and kissed it with a smile. Just as softly he spoke again.

"I like strawberries." He smiled warmly to her as well. Josephine smiled, "I like strawberries too."

King Theodore led her by the hand over to the painting he was working on. It was another landscape with rolling green hills. In this painting he had charted out space for a building or two. It was still blurry and unfinished, but she could make out a definite shape with a roof and windows. The king pointed out several parts of the picture to her all without uttering a word. She supposed the king would be explaining with great detail in his mind as he tried to point each element out to her. She focused hard and tried to take note as best as she could.

"It's a lovely painting, your highness, much like the others in here."

Wendell's father ignored her comment as he continued to silently highlight a few more things he wanted her to see. He pointed to a patch of green off to the side of the unfinished building. The color was darker with a different texture. She looked closer, feeling as if she should be seeing something significant. At first all she could see was green then one tiny red dot caught her eye. One she allowed her eyes to focus on the color, she could make out many flecks of red hidden among the dark green hues. The obvious explanation of the king's painting slapped the princess in the face. She stood up straight, trying not to laugh at herself.

"King Theodore, is this a strawberry field?" The king's countenance brightened when she understood what he had shown her. "It looks much like the one nearby with a small tavern next to it." The king was dancing from foot to foot clapping his hands with excitement.

"I like strawberries!" He cried as he celebrated.

Josephine laughed back at his excitement. "It is done very well. It looks exactly like it." The king blushed a little at her compliment. He patted his hand on her cheek as he did with his son.

"I like strawberries." He softly spoke through his smile.

Josephine returned the gesture speaking just as soft. "Thank you, I like you too."

The two of them stood for a moment as they shared a small glimpse of understanding.

Chapter 37

The prince was in awe by what just happened. Yes, his father was a bit… off… but something inside him must still be working. The king had recognized his son, understood him when he introduced the princess, and had actively tried to communicate with her. This was so far beyond anything Prince Wendell had expected; all he could do was stand there, paralyzed in shock. He was scared to move for fear that he would disrupt the flow and all this excitement would end.

Princess Josephine caught his attention, pulling him from his trance. She gave him a nod telling him to come on over. He brought up a chair and set it next to his father's stool. The king was delighted as he put his hand on his son's shoulder giving him a small, pleased smirk. It gave the prince the little extra confidence he needed to confide in his father without worry.

THE FOURTH PRINCESS

Josephine stepped away to allow the prince a little privacy with the king.

"Father, I was hoping to speak to you about Mother."

King Theodore brightened. "I like strawberries!" He started to look around the room, searching for her. The prince tried to compose him a little.

"No, she isn't here. I wanted to *ask* you about her." He emphasized his words to help him understand. The king nodded and sat up straight with his hands folded in his lap. He was focused and ready to hear what Wendell needed to say. The prince proceeded to explain all that had happened recently, starting with Princess Josephine showing up at the palace. Before he realized what he was doing he had stared discussing his goals and desires he had for the kingdom. He continued on with new ideas and values that he believed would help grow the area into a more balance place. The prince covered various topics spilling out every bit of information he always wanted to address.

Chapter

Princess Josephine gave Wendell some space due to this being the first time in years he has seen his father. She slowly worked her way around the room considering each painting in turn. They all were of the same strawberry field, but each was unique in content. Some were simple landscapes. Other paintings had workers painted in the field. One painting had carts loaded with barrels filled to the brim with berries. So many different stories painted all revolving around that field. It was beautiful to see, but Josephine couldn't help but wonder why. Of all the things he could paint, the king continues to focus on this particular strawberry field. What was so special about this one?

She had made her way to the back of the room where a massive stained glass window loomed among the covered stone walls. The picture in the glass was of the entire royal family. King and queen side by side, strong and dignified, and a younger aged prince standing in front with all his innocent grandeur. Josephine smiled at the boy while trying to imagine a young Wendell running around the castle. She lingered by the window, admiring the father and son connections the picture showed. She glanced back at the prince and could see the same loving connections between them as they talked. She delighted in the small constants of the world, and a father's love for his son is something that should never fade.

She specifically avoided looking at the queen. Princess Josephine was a forgiving woman by nature, but some situations required some extra effort and time for her to move on. The queen locking her up in the oubliette and lying to the prince about her whereabouts was one of those situations. When her eyes finally flickered over to the remainder of the window, her breath caught. Of all the emotions she could feel while looking at a representation of the queen, she would never have expected to feel excitement. Her face was young, and the lines smooth, of course. There was much about the queen portrayed here she didn't recognize. Everything from the simple robes she wore to the countenance of innocence she radiated. The glass portrait of the queen looked nothing like the ostentatious, dominating woman Josephine had encountered at the castle. However, Josephine recognized the woman in the window.

She retraced her steps through the room and found the confirmation she needed. In every painting that included the strawberry field workers there was one woman that appeared in each one. In many paintings she was no larger than a little finger in size, others were larger and more detailed, but always her. Josephine studied the glass window again to be sure. Yes, this was the queen in a younger, less troublesome time, and the king had painted her as a strawberry field worker, every time.

The prince had come to a pause in his unexpected conversation.

"She cannot go on like this. I cannot go on like this anymore." His words hovered in the air like menacing storm clouds. King Theodore sympathized with his son. Josephine could tell he wanted to say something, but in his current state, remained silent instead. She sat down next to the prince and held his hand in support. The king smiled at them. This smile held traces of nostalgia, as if he were recalling a fond, distant memory. There was also frustration. He wanted to tell them something, but didn't know how.

Josephine saw the Prince trying to mask his disappointment. There was no way King Theodore could undo everything that has happened. All she could do was hope that the king could still offer something that could help them in some way.

"You're Majesty, I find it absolutely romantic how you have painted the queen into many of your pictures." Josephine spoke quite surely, for someone who had changed the subject abruptly.

The prince looked up at her confused. The king, however, was enlivened by the comment. He immediately grabbed both of their hands and led them to another part of the room where thick drapes hung from ceiling to floor. The king drew back one of the drapes to reveal a small den hidden within the wall. It was filled with more of his paintings, with one central piece proudly displayed in the middle of the room. It was a simple profile of the queen, eyes cast down with a faint smile that curved her lips. Her hair hung loosely, cascading down around her shoulders. Her countenance was humble, yet strength shone underneath. The woman's arms were folded comfortably around a basket, as if she were on her way to work. The painting contained no embellishments of any kind, no jewels, and no fancy robes. This was the queen in her natural, true form. The prince studied the painting for a while as he tried to make sense of what the king was showing him. The princess, on the other hand, had already pieced the mystery together.

"Your highness, did the queen work in the strawberry fields?"

The king nodded in affirmation, then gazed warmly at the portrait. "I like strawberries." He whispered.

Josephine smiled in understanding. "You fell in love with her, as a strawberry field worker." The king blushed as his smile deepened. She turned towards Wendell. "Your mother was never a princess, not by blood anyway." She looked back at the king. "Is that why you requested all the strawberries from the field to be delivered to the castle, so you could see her more often." The king blushed, causing the princess to giggle. "Do you even like strawberries?" King Theodore gave her an apologetic face his eyes bearing the truth of the matter. Josephine laughed out loud at the irony of his answer.

Chapter

The prince was upset. "Why haven't you told me this before? Does anybody know the truth about mother?" The king put his finger to his lips.

Josephine's mouth gaped open. "How could you keep a secret like that? Doesn't she have any family, friends, at the very least parents that cared for her?"

The king shook his head slowly from side to side.

"No one?" The prince suspected his father was tiring and his madness was creeping back. "What, are they all dead?" he asked cynically proving his father couldn't possibly be correct. The king bowed his head solemnly in affirmation, and Prince Wendell's face grew pale from embarrassment. "Oh, no…"

Josephine covered her mouth as she gasped. "She's an orphan?" The king gave another solemn nod.

THE FOURTH PRINCESS

Wendell continued, "But, surely there are other families, friends, even a neighbor who would know her. You don't just grow up in a village and only your parents know who you are."

King Theodore turned to rummage through some pages on a nearby desk. Then waved his son over to show him what he had found. Sprawled out in from of him was a large political map that showed all the many connecting kingdoms nearby. The king was pointing to a neighboring kingdom just to the west.

"She didn't grow up in Tridith?" There was another nod of conformation from the King. Wendell continued, "Perhaps she left after he parents died and ended up here." The prince studied the map carefully. "This is King Fauntleroy's country," Prince Wendell recognized the path he had taken to find Josephine.

The king grew very excited at the mention of his friend, King Fauntleroy, and the fact that his son remembered him.

The pieces stared to make more sense to Wendell. "Father, does *HE* know about this?" Another nod in confirmation as Wendell almost laughed, "Well that explains a considerable amount about him."

The princess interrupted, "But your highness, wouldn't someone from the strawberry fields still recognize her as who she really is?"

The king patted his hand on the stone wall of the room looking forlorn.

"The walls?"

"The castle." The prince corrected as the king acknowledged him. "That's why she never leaves the castle or likes unexpected visitors. She doesn't want to be recognized." The king nodded to the prince. The answer was true, but the king did not like it at all.

Josephine tried to comfort the king. "I'm sure she came to that decision for your own sake. The truth would have stirred up some unnecessary political problems." The king nodded again, but clearly this was another fact he did not appreciate.

The prince was overwhelmed. There was too much new information about his own parents that he was trying to process. He felt a swell of compassion for his mother and the undying love his father had toward her. The prince envied him; his passion his determination. But, at the same time, there was still no excuse for his mother's behavior toward him. She has been running about with her own agenda unchecked, and he still needed to know exactly what that agenda was. Right now, he couldn't understand why his father telling him the story of how his parents got together was going to help.

The prince was frustrated. "What does this have to do with anything?" He blurted out. The princess sat him down, eager to explain.

"We have been looking at her all wrong." She started.

"You have got to be kidding me!" Prince Wendell could not believe what he was hearing.

"She doesn't want you to marry someone just like her. She wants you to marry someone better, someone who knows how to care for you and the kingdom. Someone who knows how to be a queen."

"Isn't that her?"

"Wendell, she is a woman born from humble surroundings and grew up laboring in the fields. She knows nothing about ruling a kingdom. That's why it falls on you to clean up the messes she conveniently ignores every day. You're the one who knows what you're doing, not her."

"Yes, but she must have learned…"

"From whom? Her husband perhaps, but he stared to get sick, and no one else knew the truth about her past. Who was left to turn to?"

The prince rolled his eyes as he rubbed his face with his hand. "She took over with no knowledge and no help, and no one questioned her because, she's the queen!"

Josephine nodded. "I think she's worried you are going to grow ill just like your father. If that happens she would want you married to someone capable of taking over your responsibilities and caring for you with no trouble at all. Something *she* could never do. Queen Katerina really is doing what she thinks is best."

"But she cannot continue like this. She has arranged my marriage without me, and locked you up because I chose to be with you. She lied to me so I would follow along with her masterful plan. All this under the premise that she is looking out for my best interests because I'm going to lose my mind! If I'm going crazy it is because I have her worrying too much about what could be, instead of opening her eyes to what is actually going on. Just because it happened to my father doesn't mean it's going to happen to me too!"

King Theodore and the princess listened to him solemnly.

Josephine reached out for his hand as she spoke. "You need to tell her this. She needs to know that you are in control of your life and what happens in it."

The king nodded in agreement as he rested his hand on Prince Wendell's shoulder.

The pieces of the puzzle fell perfectly into place, and the prince could see the entire picture clearly: his mother's actions, how important his assistance really was, the wisdom of his father, and the confirmation of Josephine's love along with his desire to never leave her side.

"Thank you, Father."

The prince allowed himself to linger with the king a bit longer. He originally came here so certain his father was too fragile to be of any help. Now he was keenly aware of how much strength still endured. It was, in fact, Prince Wendell who was the fragile one. The harsh reality wounded him for a moment, then the pain was replaced with an unwavering resolve. It was time to put all his frailties behind him, and draw strength from those who love him. They believed in him; it was time he believed in himself. He stood as he took Josephine by the hand.

"Come, it's time I started to lay down my own rules. Rule number one: I'm not marrying anyone but you."

He marched out of the door to find the queen, knowing exactly what needed to be done. He was no longer scared of her. Knowing the truth concerning his mother made her much less intimidating. He had found peace with his father, true love with Josephine and a small amount of clarity concerning his mother. These were things he wasn't going to allow the queen to steal away from him because of her own opinions.

Chapter

It didn't take them long to find the queen. As Wendell and Josephine tuned to cross through the throne room they were met by her and her small army of guards and attendants. Queen Katerina was startled to see Prince Wendell home again, but when she saw Princess Josephine hand in hand with him she lit up with rage!

"There she is!" bellowed the queen. "Get her!"

Half the guards ran toward her, but only three laid their hands on Josephine. The prince punched one in the face, unsheathed the guard's sword, and then kicked him to the floor. Weapon in hand, he turned to face the other two. Princess Josephine had already elbowed one of her captors in his side and knocked his nose in with the back of her head. As his grip loosened she wiggled free of the guard and kicked in the most tender spot she could find. Down went the second guard, crumpled on the floor in agony.

Wendell zeroed in on the third guard who now had a tight grasp on Josephine's wrist. She struggled to break away from his grip, but to no avail. Without hesitation, she leaned down and bit the man's knuckles as hard as she could. The prince took advantage of her distraction and knocked the guard in the side of the head with the butt of his sword. The prince quickly spun to knock the guard further away. Then Wendell positioned himself between Josephine and the rest of the guards, point of the blade out, ready for the next fool who dared to touch the princess.

The queen was fuming. "She's just one little girl! And I know my son isn't *that* good with a sword!"

The first in command spoke quickly. "Apparently he is, my queen."

Queen Katerina sighed with exasperation. "Darling!" She called out as melodious as she could. "You seem to be complicating things."

The prince's jaw dropped in shock. "I am the one complicating things? It was you who decided I needed to be married all of a sudden. It was you who couldn't handle it when I actually fell in love with someone. It was you who locked her up to hide her away from me. Mother, *you* are the one trying to take her away again! If anyone is complicating things, it is you!"

"Ungrateful child! Everything I have done has been for your best interest!"

Prince Wendell caught a glimpse of something curled up in a ball on the floor near the queen. It was hard to tell what it was by looking past the forest of legs surrounding it thanks to the guardsmen. It moved, to reveal a swollen face which looked up. Blood oozed from his nose and lip. One of his eyes was inflamed shut as the other looked directly at the prince apologetically.

"Doctor!" Josephine shouted, as she attempted to rush to his side. The princesses drew up short as the guards raised their swords, warning her not to come any closer. Wendell slowly pulled her back behind him as he tried to get a good look at his friend."

"And this? Since when is beating up an innocent fool in my best interest?"

The queen stared down her nose at the fool. "Anyone who keeps secrets from their queen deserves to be treated this way."

"And what about those who keep secrets from the Prince? Must I give you the same treatment for you to be honest with me?"

"As I said, all I have done has been for your best interest."

"Have you ever considered I have your best interest in mind too? You're my mother, I'm trying to help you to be happy as well!"

"You know nothing about what I need."

"And you know everything about my own needs?" The prince was losing his patience.

"I know handling this kingdom on your own is extensive work. So extensive, you may not be able to grasp it. I know you need a strong, capable companion who can easily take over where you cannot succeed. You need someone who knows how to command and rule a kingdom with authority and wisdom. And I know that someone is not her!"

"Then you are the only one!" Prince Wendell defied his mother with every word. "She has demonstrated all you require and more. Your mind is too clouded with hate and anger to see Princess Josephine for who she truly is."

"A coward, running from her fears!"

"A warrior, fighting every day to become better than the person she was yesterday. I will not allow you to mar her well-earned honor because of some unknown vendetta you may have. She has done nothing to you, mother. Can't you see how people are suffering because of your pride?"

"My pride is what keeps this kingdom from falling apart. My loyalty is to this kingdom! Where is your loyalty, with her?"

"My loyalty is to what's right. A kingdom cannot survive if it is lead with deceit."

"My dear boy, some of the worst things happen all because of people trying to do what is right. A little deceit can lead to more blissful times for many."

"What you're doing is wrong, mother. You've crossed the line into an evil place where demons thrive!"

The queen's face melted into concern for her son. "Oh no, it's starting already. Sweetheart, you may not know what you are saying. I think you need to lie down and allow my physicians to…"

"I AM NOT SICK!" shouted the prince. The resonating echoes from the walls quieted the queen for a moment. "You seem to think that I'm going to go mad, like my father, and your world is going to come crashing down again."

She tried to interrupt him but he continued over her words.

"I am keenly aware of everything that has been going on in this kingdom. I am the reason why this kingdom hasn't fallen apart. It is because of me, resolving unanswered problems you consistently ignore. I have been the one working to find solutions to each new conflict, ready to serve my people. And I'll be damned if I continue to sit around and allow you to withhold my own destiny, my birthright because you are waiting around for me to get sick!"

The queen hadn't listened to anything the prince said. "He is in a state of denial. Quick, restrain them both before he becomes a danger to anyone else."

The crowd of guards hesitated a fraction of a second before they obeyed the queen and advanced toward the couple. The prince held up his sword still careful to keep Josephine behind him. He had suppressed a lot of rage inside of him over the years concerning his mother's actions. Today he was ready to release it all on those who would subdue him. He knew he couldn't fight them all off, but he refused to hand over his freedom so easily. He would go down with a fight. Prince Wendell stood his ground ready to protect Princess Josephine, ready to stand up for himself and all that is right.

"Come at me!" He yelled, boldly challenging the entire room. A low roar rose up from the small army of guards as some charged forward to clash swords with the prince. Without warning, a terrible shriek of surprise pierced the room freezing everyone in their place. Wendell looked at Josephine thinking she had been the source of the sound. She was just as surprised as he was. He focused in on the queen paralyzed by her shock, pale white with terror, and hands covering her gaping mouth.

Chapter

A hush fell over the throne room as all eyes turned toward the west staircase. It was King Theodore; fully dressed in his regal robes, adorned with his numerous medals, rings and his majestic crown. He was a vision in deep blue and gold trimmed with a light fur which defined his frame to be much grander than the man Prince Wendell remembered from earlier. This man, did not look crazy; his countenance was sharp and focused. The room fell to their knees at the sight of him. Prince Wendell gave a formal bow while Princess Josephine tried to match with a flourishing courtesy. Queen Katerina still stood frozen in time, motionless, speechless. The act of breathing was a struggle for her. She never enjoyed surprises; and the king, her husband, was a definite surprise.

King Theodore slowly took in the entire room. His face softened when he looked at his beloved son, Wendell. Then, with one glance at the fool lying beaten and bleeding he hardened with anger. By the way the guards surrounding the fool cringed, they could practically feel the king's ire emanating through his gaze. Finally, his eyes settled on the queen. She was a mess. Her hair was disheveled into a stringy tangle of knots that clung around her face. Katerina's cheeks had sunken into her beautiful face. She was still a wash of surprise as he continued to consider her. The king was concerned as he slowly moved toward her. The queen's entire body trembled nervously with every step. The closer he came the more tense the room grew, everyone watching in earnest for what the king would do next.

As soon as he was close enough, he swept the queen into his powerful arms and held her, oh so tenderly, close to him. His warm embrace weakened the queen causing tears to stream down her cheeks. She returned his embrace tightly, eagerly. They lingered in their moment for a small eternity. No one had the courage to interrupt their loving display. Their arms loosened just enough for King Theodore to look at his wife face to face. A loving smile curved his lips as he smoothed down her hair. He didn't see her as anyone else in the room did. To the king, she was the most beautiful woman in the world and the most extraordinary. This woman was the one he loved more than anyone or anything. For the first time in many years the queen was able to feel that love again. Her knees went weak as the king drew her close to kiss her lips. All his love, his passion, desires combined into one glowing exchange.

The room gaped in amazement. Some cried for joy at the beautiful sight. Josephine blushed, while Wendell was transfixed by what had just happened. He saw more than a kiss. This small act had transformed the entire countenance of his mother. She no longer looked like the crazed monster he had been arguing with. She was calm, happy and absolutely lovely. She looked like a queen. It was in that moment, Wendell understood just how much power true love can have on a person. He put his arm around Josephine's waist drawing her near to him, and thankful for the true love they had for one another.

King Theodore approached Princess Josephine and bowed honorably to her. She lovingly returned the gesture to him. He took her face in his hands and gently kissed her forehead, welcoming her as a part of his family. He moved on to his son, Prince Wendell of Tridith. King Theodore smiled proudly at him practically bursting with joy. Carefully he lifted the crown from his head and fixed it firmly on Wendell's brow. With an ostentatious flourish of his robes, the King fluidly bent down to his knee to humbly bow to the new king.

The room broke out into a jubilee of chanting. "Long live King Wendell! God save the King!" Their voices showed all the honor and supplication to their king; King Wendell.

The former king rose to his full height to give his son a fatherly kiss on the cheek. He turned and collected his dear wife on his arm. Together, they left the room, hand in hand, still locked in each other's loving gaze.

Prince Wendell, now king, hurried over to the Fool to help him up from the cold, hard floor.

"Doctor, how can I help? What do you need?" He asked, anxious to do anything to ease his friend's pain.

The fool winced as he tried to laugh, but his smile remained as he answered. "Oh, it's nothing a couple days in bed can't solve." He cringed as he tried to straighten. "Maybe an herb or two to be safe."

"Anything, my friend." He answered.

King Wendell felt genuine love and a newfound understanding of the Fool. His father had been so proud of the man he had grown into. Wendell knew it was all thanks to the Fool. He had been right beside him, teaching him, ever since he entered their home. The king may have been his father in his youth, but the fool raised him to be a man. Wendell felt great love and gratitude for him because of it. He would never allow Doctor Kendell Krouss to be treated with such disrespect again. Josephine put the doctor's arm around her shoulders, intending to help him to his room.

The head guardsman stepped toward King Wendell, bowing in turn. "Your highness, what is to become of us, for following the queen's commands?"

The new king stared strongly at him, then considered the panicked, worried glances exchanged around the room.

"I believe the queen had you preparing for a wedding. Your hands are going to be full with the number of dignitaries that will be attending."

The guard looked at him skeptically. He was waiting for something much more horrible, a terrible punishment to cleanse them of their recent deeds. The prince cleared his throat which startled the guard to attention again.

"Unless, you are not up to the task, sir."

The man was still unsatisfied and concerned for the new king. "Your highness, how can we have your trust so freely, after what we have done to you and those you love?"

King Wendell spoke with authority and mercy. "You were following orders. I trust you will follow mine with as much vigor." He stared meaningfully at the man fully aware of the pain the queen's guards had inflicted on him. However, he was not going to begin his reign with more pain and suffering.

The guard quivered under the kings' intense stare. He knew he should be put to death for all that has happened, but King Wendell had shown him mercy. He would never forget this, and vowed then and there to protect the king and queen until his dying breath.

The guard smiled. "By your command, your majesty!" He shouted unable to contain his joy. The congregation of guards behind him rang up like a chorus.

"By your command, your majesty!"

Chapter

The wedding and crowning of King Wendell and Princess Josephine was one to be remembered for years to come. The kingdom was enlivened with various celebrations scattered throughout the land. Guests of all kinds flooded into the borders to share in the excitement of the new king and queen. While wedding plans were made, Wendell and Josephine took the time to visit all over the kingdom. The sight of the royal couple astounded and excited the people to no end. No longer were they a phantasmal image that emanated from the castle, silently watching over the kingdom. They now had a genuine king and queen wanting to work with them, helping them to make their land a stronger, better place. They felt loved and cared for, and many felt a revitalizing pride in their country, and their endless celebrations showed it.

For all those who attended the castle celebrations, it was indeed as astounding as the queen's invitation promised. Music rang from every corner of the palace and banquets overflowing with tasty delicacies were always within reach. Many of the guests were occupied with a continuous stream of dancing they never seemed to weary from. The former King Theodore and Queen Katerina circled among the guests to meet with all those in attendance. Queen Katerina spoke on behalf of her husband while the king shook hands and nodded on occasion. But the greatest spectacle of all was Doctor Krouss' fireworks, as he called them. Queen Josephine had helped him prepare numerous packs to be lit and launched for the celebration. The doctor was grateful for her help, but insisted she sit and watch the display at her wedding as his gift to them. The guests brimmed with awe and exhilaration with each explosion. They were continually impressed with the tiny sparks glowing in the sky that twinkled down towards them.

Gradually, the guests left to resume their responsibilities in their own countries. One by one the celebrations scattered throughout the kingdom ended, and life returned to normal again. The world seemed to slow down to a steady pace and the castle returned to its usual peaceful quiet. King Theodore and Queen Katerina had moved into a country estate to live a more calm, less strenuous life. Even the queen admitted that they would only get in the way if they remained at the castle with the newlyweds. Neither Josephine nor Wendell was upset by their decision. They were close enough to visit whenever they had the desire, but still far enough to allow them to lead the kingdom without fear of looming eyes hovering over their shoulders.

King Wendell was a standard of joy since the wedding. He was eager to resume his duties without having to be sneaky about it. Queen Josephine simply watched him work the first day overcome with awe. He slipped into the role of king with ease.

THE FOURTH PRINCESS

His confidence radiated as he executed each, well thought out, smooth, command. It was a real treat for Josephine. She felt proud to be in the same room as Wendell, let alone married to him.

All of Queen's Josephine's desires had come true after her long struggle of searching for exactly what those desires were. She was genuinely happy and knew she was exactly where she needed to be. Best of all is it was where she wanted to be.

"I have a surprise for you." King Wendell spoke to her after the usual morning business was finished.

"Since when did you have time to arrange a surprise?"

"Well, I can't really take credit for it. A messenger showed up this morning under strict orders to deliver a few items to the 'Fourth Princess'. I think you'll be interested to see who they are from."

He led her over to a sitting room set with numerous windows to allow the sunlight to fill the area. The room was warm and inviting with large overstuffed chairs and sofas. On one of the chairs sat three gifts and a letter, all wrapped up with paper and twine. Each were addressed to the *Fourth Princess*. They were from her family. Wendell and Josephine had sent formal invites out every member of her family to attend the wedding celebration. However, Josephine had not expected them to attend. They had their own kingdoms to rule and Tridith was far, far away from her home. She had expected a note or two, but not gifts, and certainly not addressed to her by the nickname she gave herself after she left home. Just how far have all those stories of her traveled? She fingered the string of a package lost in thought.

"Are you going to open them?" Wendell asked her with a smile.

Josephine blushed. "Of course."

She opened the letter from her parents first. She wasn't exactly sure what to expect; but when the letter began with an explanation of how proud they were of her and her noble pursuits, her body noticeably relaxed. She was overwhelmed by the kind words they had for her. They had understood Josephine's real talent was an understanding of the people around her. She didn't need a perfect knowledge of one single thing, just a perfect love for those around her. They knew that this beautiful love would allow her to serve and lead her kingdom in ways many would only dream of. This pleased King Ronald and Queen Laurel. Josephine would make an excellent queen who would give all she had to ensure the prosperity of her people. The princess, now queen, couldn't be happier. She found peace in their confidence that she would leave a legacy equal to that her parents had left for her. In that moment, she found her happily ever after. She was ready to tackle with fresh, unworried eyes whatever life had in store for her next.

King Wendell put his arm around his queen as she wiped a tear from her eye.

"Are you all right?" He asked.

She smiled, more brightly and dazzling than Wendell had ever seen before. "Better than all right!"

Josephine turned to the largest package to be opened. The paper fell easily to reveal an ornate, full length mirror. The frame was golden tubing twisted in every which way with precious stones of every color set among the knots. Attached was a small note from Queen Melissa to her dear, youngest sister.

Congratulations on your many adventures and your blessed marriage. Let this mirror remind you to present the best version of yourself at all times.

"It's absolutely beautiful," breathed Josephine.

Wendell nodded in agreement. "It is spectacular."

The next gift was from Queen Dianna. In moments, the room's sunlight was glistening off of eight finely crafted knives.

Each hilt was engraved with delicate scrollwork turning them more into works of art than a weapon. Nevertheless, each knife was perfectly balanced, easy to hold and sharpened to perfection.

Little Sister,

Enlivened by the many stories I have heard about you and your travels. We are excited by your recent marriage and hope you will always find joy with each other. These knives were made special for you. Let them remind you of how unique and special you are, and just as sharp. Remember me when you hold them close and never be afraid to use them whenever someone decides to underestimate you again.

Queen Dianna

Wendell's eyes stared at each knife in amazement and a hint of jealousy.

"Wow, Josephine, these are nice!" his fingers flickered towards the hilt of one knife.

Queen Josephine wittingly slapped his hand away with a warning.

"Watch it, those are mine." She smiled, daring him to try to reach for them again.

He gave her a sad, innocent look. "All of them?"

"All of them." She gave him a mysterious smile that only made him love her more.

The final package from Queen Lydia was the smallest and the most predictable. Josephine knew it was a book before she could tear away the paper. It was oversized, bound in leather with golden leafing stamped around the edges. She opened it only to be confused by the sea of blank white pages that stared back at her. She looked up at her husband who only looked back at her just as perplexed. In the front cover was message written by her eldest sister.

Best wishes on your beloved marriage to King Wendell. We have been enjoying the stories that reach us of your many achievements. Indeed, they have all helped you to become the woman that you are today. Stories like that should be recorded, so as not to be forgotten. Let them be read and re-read so you will never forget what you have done, and let them inspire you to add more extraordinary stories in the future.

"Not a bad idea. I myself have been wondering about all your many adventures." King Wendell agreed.

Josephine felt a glow rising up inside her. None of her sisters had actually said the words, but she knew they loved her immeasurably. A wave of peace enveloped her and she knew she had found her rightful place among her family. She looked up at her husband. "Are you sure you want to hear it from my perspective? These stories being told about me are much more dramatic and exciting than I remember them."

"True, but if anyone is going to tell them best, it would be you." He walked over to a writing desk nearby and held out a chair for her. She smiled as she sat down at the desk with the open book. She took a nearby pen in hand and froze before she could make a mark.

"Where do I start?"

"I find it's always best to start at the beginning."

She stared at the blank page as her memories started to spin in her mind. She gave a large toothy grin at the page and started to scribble to keep up with the words that flowed so freely.

Once upon a time there was a beautiful kingdom. It was ruled by a king who was extremely wise, and a queen who was absolutely lovely.

THE FOURTH PRINCESS

They had four beautiful princesses. The eldest was clever in all things, the next was strong in will and might, and the third was beautiful beyond all comprehension. There was also the littlest princess among them known as the Fourth Princess...

www.ingramcontent.com/pod-product-compliance
Lightning Source LLC
LaVergne TN
LVHW021047100526
838202LV00079B/4666